About the Author

Nathan Dylan Goodwin was born and raised in Hastings, East Sussex. Schooled in the town, he then completed a Bachelor of Arts degree in Radio, Film and Television, followed by a Master of Arts Degree in Creative Writing at Canterbury Christ Church University. A member of the Society of Authors, he has completed a number of successful local history books about Hastings, as well as other works of fiction in this series; other interests include reading, photography, skiing, travelling and of course, genealogy. He is a member of the Guild of One-Name Studies and the Society of Genealogists, as well as being a member of the Sussex Family History Group, the Norfolk Family History Society, the Kent Family History Society and the Hastings and Rother Family History Society. He lives in Kent with his partner and young son.

BY THE SAME AUTHOR

nonfiction:
Hastings at War 1939-1945 (2005)
Hastings Wartime Memories and Photographs (2008)
Hastings & St Leonards Through Time (2010)
Around Battle Through Time (2012)

fiction
(The Forensic Genealogist series):
Hiding the Past (2013)
The Lost Ancestor (2014)
The Orange Lilies (2014) – *A Morton Farrier novella*
The America Ground (2015)
The Spyglass File (2016)

The Orange Lilies
by Nathan Dylan Goodwin

This book is dedicated to the thousands of fallen men of the Royal Sussex Regiment 1914-1918, including two members of my own family:

Lance Corporal James Dengate

1st Battalion, Royal Sussex Regiment, 1897 - 14 September 1917, Karachi, Pakistan

Private James Ernest Dengate

16th Battalion, Royal Sussex Regiment, 1889 - 21 September 1918, Cambrai, France

www.everymanremembered.org

'On that fateful day, Tuesday 4th August, 1914, one of the many orders sent out by telegram from the War Office under the requirements of 'The War Book' was addressed to the Commanding Officer, 2nd Battalion The Royal Sussex Regiment, Battalion Headquarters, Inkerman Barracks, Woking, Surrey. The telegram contained one stark and momentous word: 'Mobilise'.'

We Won't be Druv—The Royal Sussex Regiment on the Western Front 1914-1918

Prologue

12th August 1914, The Solent, off Southampton, England

The *S.S. Agapenor*, a 455 foot-long cargo vessel, dramatically cut through the inky swells of the Solent, which was tonight unusually busy. It was almost two am and most of its cargo—disparate regiments comprising a part of the British Expeditionary Force—was asleep in whatever space could be found. An earlier drama, when the steam ship had collided with another vessel shortly after departing Southampton, had been quickly forgotten. The ship had been bruised but had continued her voyage nonetheless.

Charles Ernest Farrier could not sleep. It was windowless and airless; he could have been anywhere. But he wasn't anywhere, he was just days, maybe even hours away from war. He was in an area of the cargo hold somewhere deep below deck with some of his closest friends: Leonard Sageman, David Dowd, Frank Eccles, Tom Trussler, Arthur Jarret—all pals who had spent the last few months in close quarters with each other. This was no exception. The Second Battalion of the Royal Sussex Regiment, in which Charles served as a private, was required urgently at the front. The German army, like an insatiable plague of locusts, had swarmed through Belgium and on into France. Back in England, calls for men to volunteer to fight had been answered in their thousands. At twenty-four years of age, Charles had already had training as a regular soldier; he felt somewhere close to ready to fight but knew that the training given to new recruits would be rushed, inadequate and potentially fatal. Despite his training, Charles still felt unprepared. He knew that the battleground that they faced would be nothing like the sleepy training grounds at Inkerman Barracks in Woking, where the regiment had spent the summer. There, in neat rows of bell-tented camps set in the undulating hills of the English countryside, they had undertaken rigorous route marches, assault courses and rifle shooting.

'You okay, Charlie?' a low voice whispered from beside him. Despite the pitch black, he knew that the voice had come from Leonard, his best friend, who was slumped up against him. Several years ago, the pair of them had arrived on the Sussex coast in search of work, leaving behind them the poor districts of Lambeth that had

1

taken so many members of their respective families, including their parents, to an early grave. When their searches had failed to alleviate their poverty, together, in 1910, they had enlisted to become regular soldiers.

'Just can't sleep. Thinking about home.'

Leonard patted his arm. 'Best thing you can do is try not to think of home—that's what I'm trying to do. Put your energy into preparing to fight this bloody war.'

'Yeah,' Charles said, absent-mindedly. It was easier for Leonard, he had no real family left to speak of but Charles had a wife and a new son to think about.

Charles heard the soft sound of Leonard's head sagging into his hessian kitbag and found himself alone once again, with only the darkness and his own thoughts for company. He fished about in his pocket and pulled out his most precious possession: the photograph of his wife, Nellie and his six-week-old son, Alfred. Drawing the photograph right up to his face so that it rested on the end of his nose, Charles tried desperately to make out any features on the picture, but he saw nothing. He closed his eyes and allowed his mind to reproduce the image of them on the day that the photograph had been taken. They had been sitting in smart, fashionable clothes, which had been borrowed from a neighbour, and had sat smiling for the photographer.

Charles gently kissed the photograph, hoping that it wouldn't be too long until they were reunited. But his fate rested in the hands of others.

War was spreading through Europe, like an invasive deathly smog.

And he was sailing right towards it.

Chapter One

21ˢᵗ December 2014, Cornwall, England

Morton Farrier was apprehensive. He was cruising down the A30 in his red Mini and had just passed the 'Welcome to Cornwall' sign. It was one of the few places outside of his home county of Sussex which would usually evoke in him a feeling of warm syrupy comfort. It was the place of perfect childhood family holidays: camping trips to the Lizard Peninsular with his mum, dad and younger brother, Jeremy. It was a period of blissful childhood ignorance for him. Today, however, the shrinking gap between him and his destination only increased his anxiety.

'Stop biting your nails,' Juliette said, reaching across from the passenger seat and forcibly removing his fingers from his mouth. She clamped his hand down under hers. 'What's up?'

Morton breathed out slowly and gave Juliette's hand a gentle squeeze. 'Just getting nervous about seeing her, that's all.' He turned to her and grimaced.

Juliette looked at him with a reassuring smile. 'It's only natural, but you do need to try and relax or you're not going to have a good Christmas.'

'I know,' he answered flatly.

'Think how nervous *she'll* be feeling,' Juliette added.

He had thought about that already and that only made his apprehension worse, as if shouldering some of *her* burden himself might have made the situation that he was about to face somehow easier. 'Do you think we're doing the right thing in coming down here?'

'Definitely,' she said, staring at Morton's profile. 'This issue has plagued you since you were sixteen. It's time you put it to bed.'

'If only it were that simple,' he murmured, briefly turning so that their eyes locked. He had been told by his father that he was adopted twenty-four years ago, yet it felt like only a matter of weeks had passed since then, and simultaneously like it was something that he had always known. Ever since that day he had had a veritable army of conflicting thoughts and emotions constantly battling in his head. Sometimes he had wanted to know the truth about his past, other times he resolutely did not. Age and maturity now told him that those occasions when he did *not* want to know his real past were simply defence mechanisms that his spurned brain had created to challenge the reality that he was unwanted. Last year that particular conflict had come to a resolution when his father had informed Morton that his real mother was actually his Aunty Margaret—his father's sister. One result from that discovery was that slowly since that day, Morton had begun to accept and properly assume his surname, Farrier. It was, after all, his mother's maiden name—her name at the point of his birth. It had suddenly become less random like his Christian name and more sturdy and real; he finally belonged to a family tree with roots creeping and pervading into the depths of history. As a forensic genealogist, he found it a revealing moment to know that he had ancestors—*real* ancestors with stories waiting to be told.

The news that his Aunty Margaret was actually his mother had been hastily followed by the unpalatable revelation that she had been raped at the age of sixteen. As hard as he had tried, Morton couldn't escape the ever-present cloud of knowledge that he owed fifty percent of his DNA to someone capable of such a heinous crime.

And now, here he was, about to have his first meeting with his Aunty Margaret since she had been made aware that Morton now knew of his true parentage.

'How much further?' Juliette asked, moving uncomfortably in her seat.

'About another hour and a half. Why don't you try and rest for a bit?'

Juliette muttered her agreement and tried to achieve as close to a foetal position as the seat would allow.

Within a few minutes, Morton could hear the deep gentle inhalation and exhalation, which signalled that she had achieved sleep, despite her squashed appearance. Morton tried to shift his thoughts from the looming meeting. His eyes followed the steady, inevitable stream of traffic that blighted the main arteries into Cornwall once the motorway had fizzled out.

After a while, the traffic thinned and the gaps between the houses began to grow. The Mini zipped through picturesque rolling green hills lined with low hedges and stone walls, so characteristic of Cornwall. When the first iconic tin mine tower appeared at the side of the road, in striking red brick and granite, Morton knew that he was in the heart of Cornwall and fast approaching his biological mother.

A swollen orange sun clung to the distant horizon, as he pushed further down into the Lizard Peninsular, the roads twisting, turning and narrowing. High gorse hedges and great swathes of decaying brown bracken became a common sight at the side of the road.

Finally, he passed a small white sign with a thin black border and lettering announcing the village name of 'Cadgwith'. Morton couldn't help but let out a small gasp.

Juliette stirred, rubbed her eyes and sat up. 'What's the matter?' she asked, glancing from Morton to the deserted country lane, expecting to see something noteworthy.

'Nothing, sorry. We're here, is all,' Morton breathed uneasily. If he had ever felt more nervous than he did right now, then he couldn't bring the occasion to mind.

Juliette stretched out and gently patted his leg. 'Jolly good—I'm starving. Wow—look at all those cottages! They're stunning.'

Morton knew that she was trying to pacify him with joviality and distraction, but it hadn't worked.

He tucked his car into a tight space on a ramshackle pea-beach driveway, the Mini's front bumper resting inches from a number-plate-style plaque that said 'SEA VIEW'. Morton switched off the engine and held his breath. The car was silent. The village was silent. It seemed at that moment that all of Cornwall was silent, as if trying to placate his apprehension.

He exhaled and looked at Juliette. *Thank God you're here,* he thought. He wouldn't have come alone—he didn't feel emotionally strong enough. He knew, for various reasons, that this break to Cornwall would be a significant juncture in his life.

It was time to face the past.

His past.

Morton turned to Juliette. 'Come on, let's do it.'

He turned to open his door but she pulled him back. 'Morton, try and relax and let things unfold naturally—don't force it or it could all go pear-shaped.'

He nodded and kissed her on the lips. She was right. If he went blundering in headfirst, it could all go horribly wrong and potentially send unbridgeable fault lines through the Farrier family. In his line of work diplomacy and tact were important skills when dealing with clients. *That's what I need to do,* he thought, *step back and treat this as a genealogical case.* Just the thought of disconnecting himself slightly from the situation gave him a vague notion of confidence. He stepped out of the car and hauled their luggage from the boot.

Dragging one case each behind them, the pair walked briskly, in defiance of a chilly Atlantic wind. Hand in hand, they strode towards three whitewashed cottages, which had been cut into the hill.

Sea View was the first cottage on the path. At the height of summer the house embodied all the traits of a traditional English home: a gloriously scented honeysuckle rambled over the porch; vibrant pink roses and orange lilies splayed across the front walls, and an array of cottage garden flowers blossomed in the front garden. Today, in the middle of winter, the flora had been reduced to only the hardiest plants capable of fighting against the spiteful sea air.

'Here we are,' Morton said.

Juliette switched her attention to the cove over which the house looked. 'What a view,' she said. 'Amazing.'

'I told you it was nice,' Morton said, placing his arm over her shoulder and pulling her tightly to him. 'I could so easily live here.'

'I don't think I would ever leave the house if I could wake up to that every day.'

'Not so great in a storm,' a voice suddenly chimed from behind them.

The pair turned and there in the porch, with a wide grin on her face, was Margaret. She was exactly the same as the last time Morton had seen her. To him, she was one of those people who rarely changed or aged. She stood in a flowery dress, hair frizzy and white, slightly plump from her fondness for homemade cakes, with a happy glowing face. If she was feeling as nervous as Morton then she certainly wasn't showing it. 'Well, don't just stand there, come and give your Aunty Margaret a big cuddle.'

Morton grinned and embraced her.

He closed his eyes and held her tightly. The usual feelings of sugary warmth quickly gave way to an unfamiliar sensation. *He was holding his mother. His own, biological mother.* It was a day that he had feared, dreaded and longed for desperately. In a strange kind of way, he was at home. His feelings only served to underline how uncomfortable he had often felt in his father's house; an irreconcilable juxtaposition.

Morton pulled back from the hug when he felt his eyes begin to moisten. 'Aunty Margaret, this is Juliette. Juliette, this is Aunty Margaret.'

The two women smiled and instinctively hugged each other.

'It's lovely to finally meet you, Juliette.'

'You too—he talks about you all the time,' Juliette said.

6

'Oh dear,' Aunty Margaret said, turning to go inside the house. 'Let's get in out of the cold.'

They stepped into a dim, surprisingly spacious lounge with a low-beamed ceiling and roaring open fire. A fat Norse pine was handsomely adorned with fairy lights, tinsel and assorted Christmas decorations.

'What a lovely place,' Juliette remarked.

'It's not bad,' Aunty Margaret said. 'Could do with a lick of paint here and there, but it's home. Right, I expect you're gasping for a drink, aren't you? Tea? Coffee? Something stronger?'

'Tea would be lovely, please,' Juliette answered.

'Coffee, please,' Morton added, taking stock of the room. It was just as he had remembered it; very little had changed. The addition of the Christmas tree and decorations only made it seem more homely.

'You two take a seat and I'll fetch the drinks,' she said, momentarily disappearing from view before her head popped around the corner. 'Actually, why don't I show you your rooms, then you can come and go as you please.'

Morton and Juliette followed her up a narrow wooden staircase to a landing offering four doors. Morton's previous childhood visits had always meant the eviction of one of his cousins from their bedroom, but now Jess and Danielle had both left home, so he guessed their old rooms would now be vacant.

'The guest suite,' Aunty Margaret said, lifting a black iron latch and swinging wide the door.

'Danielle's old room,' Morton recalled.

'That's right. Well, it still is when she returns from her jaunts overseas.' She turned to Juliette and said, 'She's an airhostess or whatever you call them—flight attendant. Anyway, for the next five days it's all yours. Free of charge!'

Typical of a fifteenth-century dwelling, the bedroom offered no right angles, straight walls or level ceilings or floors, but it did offer a great deal of quirky charm.

Juliette stooped down to look through the window. She slowly took in the breathtaking views of the small cove nestled between two hills, upon which the village had relied for centuries. 'Wow,' she said. 'I just can't get over that view.'

'I'll leave you to enjoy it. I've cleared some space in the wardrobe, so if you want to unpack, you can. When you're ready, come downstairs and we'll have a catch up.'

'Thanks, Aunty Margaret,' Morton said, gently squeezing her arm.

'She's so lovely,' Juliette enthused when the creaking stairs told her that Margaret was out of earshot. 'And this place. And this village. *Why* have you never brought me here before?'

Morton pulled a *you know why* face.

'I meant *before* your dad told you.'

Morton shrugged, biting his fingernails. 'Come on, let's get downstairs.'

Juliette wrestled his fingers out of his mouth again. '*Relax*. It's supposed to be a mini-holiday, not an ordeal. Here, help me unpack first.'

Half an hour later, Morton and Juliette were sitting on a battered green sofa in front of the open fire sipping tea and eating homemade scones. Margaret had brought Morton up to date with news about her two daughters and their latest exploits. Much to his disappointment, neither would be coming home for Christmas, although Morton wasn't sure if Margaret had requested that they stay away. He had no idea if they knew that he was in fact their half-brother and not their first cousin, as they had always believed.

As Morton and Juliette tucked into their food and drink, the lull in the conversation grew to a period of near-silence. Only the crackling fire contributed to the sound in the lounge.

Morton swallowed down a mouthful of coffee, wondering how best to address the elephant in the room. As always seemed to happen to him at such moments, his brain refused to find a way to navigate the dangerous and uncharted territory into which he was about to sail. As he sipped at his drink, he selected then discarded words with which to open his sentence. Nothing sounded right. *Maybe there are no words*, Morton wondered. He took a fleeting glance at his Aunty Margaret. She was slumped comfortably back in the armchair, hands knitted together over her apron with a smile on her face, staring into the fire. She was a lovely, simple woman. Not simple in her intelligence, just simple in her life. There had never been any complications or arguments or problems with Margaret. Her life was just enviously simple. He marvelled at her perpetual sunniness. But was she really not feeling the same thing—struggling to verbalise her forty-year secret, which she must have hoped would go with her to the grave? An awful feeling washed over him. What if she had no intention of discussing his past with him? If she were anything like Morton's father—her brother—then difficult situations would be swiftly dealt with by brushing them under the carpet and pretending that they didn't exist.

Margaret turned to face him. 'I think I just heard your Uncle Jim's car. Thought he was taking his time. Expect he got side-tracked at the pub, knowing him,' she said with a laugh. 'Here he is, now.'

Morton and Juliette stood and followed Margaret towards the door as it swung open.

'Ahoy, me old Sussex hearties!' Jim exclaimed in his thick Cornish accent, stepping heavy boots into the lounge. He was a giant bear of a man—red ruddy complexion and tanned leathery skin, revealing a lifetime spent on fishing boats. He threw a large meaty hand in Morton's direction. 'Nephew!'

Morton grinned. 'Hi, Uncle Jim. This is Juliette.'

Jim offered his hand to her. 'Pleased to make your acquaintance, young lady.' He turned to face Morton. 'You kept this little treasure hidden nicely, didn't you? She don't look like a copper, does she?'

'I'll take that as a compliment,' Juliette said with a laugh.

'Well, just you keep on your best behaviour, James Daynes, and you'll be alright.'

Jim peeled off a thick wax jacket. 'Seriously, though, it's lovely to have you both here. We've been looking forward to it, haven't we, Margaret?'

'Absolutely. Well, all this sitting down won't do. I'd best get the dinner on. You two make yourselves at home. Stick the television on if you fancy.'

'Do you need a hand at all?' Morton asked hopefully, wondering if she needed it to be just the two of them in order to talk candidly.

'I can manage fine, thanks. You just relax.'

Morton was disappointed, but sat back down and entered into conversation with his Uncle Jim, accepting that the matter was not about to be discussed.

After a full roast dinner had been devoured and cleaned up, Morton and Juliette sat back in front of the fire with Margaret and Jim. The dinner table conversation had danced and skirted neatly around the topic that Morton had most wanted to speak about, raising his fretfulness all the more.

Jim pressed the television remote control exaggeratedly. 'Christ, there's nothing on. Christmas television used to be cracking, now it's all a load of drivel and repeats. Two documentaries on at the same time

9

about the bloody Christmas Truce of 1914. Two! Bit heavy for my liking—not very Christmassy. Anyone want to watch either of them?'

'I don't mind what we watch,' Juliette answered diplomatically.

Margaret looked indifferent. 'Might see Grandad Farrier or Grandad Len on there—they were both fighting in 1914. God only knows if they had a truce or not. Probably not if Grandad Farrier was like the other stubborn men in the family!'

Morton looked up as a wave of guilt flashed through his mind. How could a forensic genealogist know so little—nothing in fact—of his own family history? Since discovering his bone fide connection to the Farrier family he had intended to begin research but other paid cases kept taking precedence. He determined there and then to set aside some time next year to research his own family tree. Morton zoned back into the room. Juliette and Jim were in a conversation about Christmas television, so Morton turned to his Aunty Margaret. 'Do you not know what happened to your grandfather in the war, then?'

Aunty Margaret turned her nose up. 'Not much. It's a bit of a mystery, really—no photos of him or information about him; it's like he never existed. I mean, I *do* understand why he's been forgotten: he died fairly early on in the war and my dad never knew him—he was born around the same time his father was killed. My granny remarried after the war—a chap called Len who was a friend of Grandad Farrier's. Lovely man, Len was, too. I've got a photo somewhere of him in his uniform and some old postcards and letters he sent back from a prisoner-of-war camp, but nothing from Grandad Farrier. Funnily enough, I've been thinking about him recently, what with all this hundred-year anniversary stuff going on. Surely *you* can find out what happened to him?'

'Possibly,' Morton said, running his fingers through his hair. 'The problem is that about sixty percent of service records for soldiers who served in World War One were destroyed in a bombing raid in World War Two when the War Office was hit.'

'Oh, that's a pity,' Aunty Margaret lamented. 'I was hoping you might be able to tell me a bit more about them.'

Morton shot a look at Juliette.

'Go and get it,' she said with a sigh.

Morton grinned. He had promised her that, despite bringing his laptop with him, he wouldn't be working. *This isn't really work, though,* he reasoned, *it's my family.* Besides which, it might be just the hook that he

10

needed to get his Aunty Margaret talking. 'I'll just fetch my laptop and see what I can find.'

'Jolly good,' Margaret said, rubbing her hands with excitement.

Moments later, Morton returned carrying his Mac. He sat down beside Margaret and opened up a web browser.

'All at the click of a button,' Margaret mused, as she watched Morton tapping at the keyboard.

'Not everything—but a lot,' he replied. 'I realise this question is a little ironic coming from me, but what was your grandfather's name?'

'Charles Ernest Farrier,' came the reply.

Charles Ernest Farrier. His great grandfather. He suddenly felt callous and somehow stupid for not even knowing his own great grandfather's name.

With Margaret looking keenly over his shoulder, Morton started with the Commonwealth War Graves Commission website, which listed all casualties of the First and Second World Wars. A moment later, his great grandfather's name, in bold capital letters headed the top of the screen. Below it, were the details pertaining to his death.

Rank: Private
Date of death: 26/12/14
Regiment/Service: Royal Sussex Regiment, 2nd Bn.
Awards: None
Panel Reference: Panel 20 and 21
Memorial: Le Touret Memorial

'Gosh, he didn't last long, did he? Poor chap,' Margaret said. 'Where's Le Touret?'

'Pas de Calais,' Morton answered, trying to assimilate the information in front of him. It was a strange haunting feeling for him to be looking at records for his own family. He had used the CWGC website countless times to help his clients find their lost ancestors, but here he was, looking at the death date of his own great grandfather. As he clicked to view the details of the cemetery in Le Touret, which commemorated more than 13,400 soldiers, he made his mind up to pay a visit to the cemetery at some point in the future.

Morton pulled out his trusty notepad and pen from his laptop bag and jotted down the information onscreen. On the next page he began to construct a basic tree for the Farrier family. 'Do you know Charles's wife's name?' he asked Margaret.

'Nellie,' she answered. 'I can't recall her maiden name, though.'

'I can find that easily enough,' Morton responded, scribbling her name beside Charles's. 'And their son, Alfred, was your father?'

'That's right—your grandad. He was only born in June 1914, so he definitely wouldn't have known his dad—poor soul. No wonder he never spoke of him.'

'Charles can't have been very old when he died,' Morton said.

'No, in his twenties—older than a lot of those poor soldiers, though.'

'Right,' Morton said, adding the details to his notepad. 'With a bit of luck we can find Charles's MIC,' Morton said, opening up a new browser and heading to the Ancestry website.

'His what?' Margaret said with a chuckle.

'Medal Index Card—a good starting point for World War One records.'

'Off you go, then!'

Morton located the online records for World War One and entered Charles's name into the search box. Of the two available records listed, Morton clicked to view Charles's Medal Index Card. Seconds later, a salmon-coloured scan with blue handwritten ink appeared onscreen.

'More code!' Margaret lamented, when she saw the baffling array of letters and numbers presented. She flung her hands up. 'You'll have to decipher it for me, Morton.'

Morton smiled. 'I'll give it my best shot. Right. Obviously his name, Charles Ernest Farrier, you can read. He was in the second battalion of the Royal Sussex Regiment, number 7512. He was a private. He was awarded the Victory Medal, British War Medal and 1914 Star.'

'What are all those letters and numbers for, then?'

'They tell you where his name is entered on the medal roll.'

'Can we look that up?' she asked hopefully.

Morton shook his head. 'It's only available at The National Archives in Kew. I've searched it before but most of the time it doesn't give any more information than the Medal Index Card. I'll take a look, though, next time I'm up there.'

Morton ran his finger down the card. The section marked 'Theatre of War first served in' had been left blank. Below it, however, the part marked *Date of entry therein* had been entered as '12-8-14'.

'Look, he went out on the 12th August 1914, which means that he was a regular soldier—not volunteered or conscripted.'

'*K in A* 26th December 1914?' she asked.

'Killed in action.'

'Course it is!' Margaret said.

Morton scribbled down the new information then reverted back to the list of records available for Charles. He next clicked on 'UK Soldiers Died In The Great War, 1914-1919'.

Name: Charles Farrier
Birth Place: Lambeth, London
Birth Date: 2 Feb 1890
Death Date: 26 Dec 1914
Death Place: British Expeditionary Force
Enlistment Place: Chichester
Rank: Private
Regiment: Royal Sussex Regiment
Battalion: 2nd Battalion
Regimental Number: L/7512
Type of Casualty: Killed in Action
Theatre of War: Western European Theatre

'Place of death, British Expeditionary Force?' Margaret said incredulously. 'Is that a mistake?'

'No, that's a blanket, cover-all term the military used since so many casualties were never found.'

Aunty Margaret shook her head. 'So was Charles not found, then?'

'Er...hang on,' Morton answered, switching back to the Commonwealth War Graves Commission website. 'No. Panel 20 and 21 means he was one of God knows how many men whose bodies were never found.'

Both Morton and Margaret paused whilst they digested this information.

'Poor Granny. Imagine being told your husband's been killed in action but there's no body to bury, no funeral service, no grave to mourn at.' She took a deep, reflective breath. 'We don't know we're born.'

'Indeed,' Morton agreed. 'That's all Ancestry seem to have on his military career. Let me just check Findmypast.' With a few quick clicks, Morton was presented with three records for Charles. Two were identical to those already searched. He clicked the third—'British Army

13

Service Records 1760-1915' and waited as a four-page document loaded: Army Form E.504. 'It's Charles's militia attestation form.'

'And what's that then, when it's at home? Looks like there's a lot on there.'

'It's basically his enlistment papers. Usual questions, like name, age, address,' Morton said, scanning down the page for additional information pertaining to his great grandfather's military career. 'So, it says he was a painter and decorator prior to joining up. He was married, with one child under fourteen. He'd never been in prison…'

'I should hope not!' Margaret interrupted with a laugh.

'He signed up for six years in 1910…poor bloke can't have had a clue what would happen four years down the line.' Morton clicked onto the next page. 'This is his personal information—I always find this helps me to better imagine what they looked like.'

Margaret leant forward and squinted at the screen.

Apparent age: 20 years 3 months
Height: 5 feet 10 inches
Weight: 10 stone 6 lbs
Chest measurement minimum: 29 inches
Chest measurement maximum: 32 inches
Complexion: Fresh
Eyes: Brown
Hair: Light brown
Religious denomination: Wesleyan
Distinctive marks, and marks indicating congenital peculiarities or previous disease: scar on right forearm

From the physical description in front of him, Morton could have been looking at his own details at the age of twenty-four.

'Gosh, we've found a lot already. Is there more to be unearthed?'

'Possibly. There's a lot being digitised right now. Some unit war diaries are already online but they don't usually mention individual soldiers by name.'

'Still, worth a look,' Margaret said. 'I'd love to know more.'

The credits of the programme which Juliette and Jim had been watching rolled, spurring a flurry of yawns and stretches.

'Anyone want the TV on?' Jim asked.

'Not for me, thanks,' Juliette answered. 'Think I'm about ready for bed. How are you two getting on?' she asked, wandering over towards Morton and Margaret.

'It's just amazing what's out there,' Margaret replied, shaking her head in disbelief. 'You wouldn't credit what he's found about my grandfather this evening. So interesting!'

'Oh, believe me, I know what he's like with his research,' Juliette said with a grin. 'On that note, I'm off to bed. You coming up?'

'Yes, I think we'll call it a day, don't you, Aunty Margaret?'

'Only if we can carry on tomorrow.'

'Fine by me,' Morton answered, shutting the lid on his laptop. Morton said goodnight and headed up to the bedroom.

'Sounded like you two were getting on pretty well,' Juliette whispered, having pushed the bedroom door shut.

Morton smiled and sat down on the edge of the bed and began to undress. 'Yeah, it's nice—just like old times, really. It's been lovely finding out about my own family history for once, but I have this awful feeling that she doesn't want to talk about what I've come here to talk about. I can just see the two of us researching her grandfather's military career for all of Christmas, then we'll head home having missed our opportunity.'

'I'm sure she's just waiting for the right time,' Juliette said quietly. 'She might just be showing you that nothing's changed. For all you know, she might be thinking that you're worried that she'll jump into your mum's place. She's probably just letting you know that she's still the same Aunty Margaret that she always has been.'

Morton sighed. 'Let's hope so. I don't want things to change between us, but I *do* want to discuss it.'

'Let's see what tomorrow brings, shall we?' Juliette said, gently stroking his hair. 'Come on, let's get some sleep.'

Morton put his night t-shirt and boxer shorts on and slipped into bed beside Juliette. He switched off the light, kissed her goodnight and began to replay all the information that he had just learnt about his great grandfather. In just a few short hours, Morton had learned a great deal about Charles. Having seen and read so much about the Great War, Morton wondered at what horrors Charles had seen and, ultimately, what had taken his life on the 26th December 1914.

Chapter Two

21st December 1914, Hazebrouck, Northern France

Just a few months ago, seven am in Hazebrouck, Central Square would have contained only a handful of French men and women innocuously going about their daily lives, all unaware of the destructive war clouds looming in the distance. The heady aromas of fresh coffee and hot breads would have seeped into the air over the cobbled square, enticing passers-by on their way to work. Today, however, with most of the buildings overlooking the square solemn and all but closed down, the lack of locals was compensated for by the full complement of the Second Battalion of the Royal Sussex Regiment. They were standing, like a neatly sewn khaki blanket, in ordered rows waiting to board a fleet of motorbuses which had been requisitioned from England. The buses, with their hastily boarded-up windows and matching khaki paint, had been sent in order to move troops quickly and efficiently to the frontline. It was the second time that the Battalion had been in Hazebrouck. On the first occasion, they had marched there in a blizzard, arriving on the 19th November. They had stayed there for the remainder of the month, whilst reinforcements were brought in. Such were the losses experienced by the Battalion in the opening weeks of the war, that Charles now barely recognised the Battalion of old.

'Reckon we'll get on this *Ole Bill,*' Leonard whispered to Charles.

'Let's hope so, I just want to get on with it,' he answered quietly, as he watched one motorbus crammed with soldiers being replaced swiftly by an empty one.

'Next lot, get a move on,' barked Sergeant Buggler.

The line surged forward and Leonard, followed by Charles, climbed the external steps to the open top-deck seating.

'More, more!' Buggler shouted. 'Squash up—you're not on a bloody sight-seeing tour.'

Charles took the next available seat beside Frank Eccles, with Leonard shoved to his right. The bus filled quickly, with men taking every inch of available space.

Suddenly, the bus lurched forward and they were on their way, returning to the front.

Some of the men around him used the opportunity to snatch a few minutes' rest, others chatted quietly. There was something akin to a nervous ripple that had been quietly buzzing around the Battalion since they had been told that they were heading back to the front to relieve the Seaforth Highlanders. It was in stark contrast to their early days, when excitement and anticipation at finally seeing action had dominated every conversation. But their first days were filled with endless marching, day after day. In late August, the Battalion had spearheaded the British Expeditionary Force's retreat from Mons. More marching—*away* from the enemy. Endless hours of marching. Men dropping by the roadside, exhausted. By the end of August, his comrades were beginning to ask each other and their superiors when would they turn and fight the enemy, as they had been trained to do? When the retreat was finally over, the Battalion had marched sixty miles in sixty-five hours. The men had been beyond shattered.

The Battalion's first sighting of the enemy had been on the 10th September. On high ground near the village of Priez, a line of German soldiers had come into view, sending a buzz of excitement through the men like a bolt of electricity, as they had marched through the village with a newfound sense of adventure and purpose, seemingly oblivious to the thick torrents of rain that had lashed down on them. They had been greeted on the other side of the village by unexpectedly heavy fire, subjecting the Battalion to its first substantial losses; the skirmish had left seventeen dead and eighty-three injured. That night, sheltered in their billets in the town of Paissy, the four Battalion companies had been subdued; their initial bravado had yielded to the realities of war: their comrades and friends were lying dead in a French field. Four days later and the Battalion was hit again by severe losses. Whilst occupying high ground above Vendresse, the Battalion had managed to take a group of two hundred and fifty German soldiers by surprise. The Germans had quickly surrendered under a white flag and were taken prisoner. It was whilst being marched away that other German soldiers randomly opened fire, killing several men, including their own. The fighting had continued and the Battalion had been ordered to dig itself into trenches and hold their position. Among the one hundred and fourteen missing, wounded and dead of the Second Battalion was David Dowd, a close friend of Charles's. He had suffered a fatal bullet wound to the head and Charles had watched helplessly as he quietly slipped away. There had been no time to bury him. No time for grieving.

'What you thinking about, Charlie?' Leonard asked.

'Nothing,' Charles answered. 'Just wondering what we're going back to. More wet and muddy trenches. It's not exactly the open warfare we trained for, is it?'

Leonard laughed. 'I don't know what you mean—it's exactly like the gentle, rolling hills of Woking and the English countryside.'

'I just hope they train the poor blighters answering Kitchener's call-up,' Charles said sombrely. The war had changed direction in mid-September. The shelling, sniping and artillery bombardment continued, but taking place in an ever-expanding warren of trenches, stretching their way tentacle-like through the fields of Europe. Sightings of the enemy diminished to the point that new recruits, drawn up from the territorials to replace the fallen, had *never* actually seen them. But the death and destruction had continued. More and more familiar faces had disappeared into the French soil. There had been a glimmer of hope when, on the 25th October, they had marched into Belgium. Eager fresh eyes searched the city for sightings of the enemy, but they weren't to be found. After one night comfortably billeted within the city walls, the following day they had to march to their destination: Château Wood, two miles outside of Ypres. Any hope of trench warfare being over was blighted when the Battalion found themselves entrenched in Polygon Wood, where men and horses were killed in great numbers and the Battalion was forced to retreat back to Château Wood.

'Here we are,' Frank said cheerfully, jolting Charles from his thoughts.

In a vast expanse of flat countryside, dominated by large tracts of empty brown fields and no obvious landmarks, the motorbus drew to a stop.

Charles observed the swelling mass of khaki in a nearby field, as the four companies comprising the Battalion began to regroup. He stood and made his way down the stairs and off the bus.

As he stepped down onto the soggy soil, Charles noticed for the first time the sporadic dull thudding of shells landing somewhere near the distant village of Le Touret—precisely where they were heading.

Chapter Three

Nellie Farrier, dressed in a long red coat and matching hat, cut a striking figure in the gloom of the cliff edge. It was bitterly, bitingly cold as she stood, hands tightly clasped to the pram, staring into the endless dreariness of the English Channel, where sea and sky met seamlessly. She was perched at the top of a rolling chalk downland on the tail-end of the South Downs. Waiting and listening. She glanced down into the pram. Wrapped up like a tiny doll, her son, Alfred slept in blissful ignorance of the darkness that was ravaging the continent.

Then she heard it; the sound that she had so often, almost daily, climbed the steep ascent from the dirty backstreets of Eastbourne to hear: the agonising thump and thud of heavy artillery pounding French soil, indiscriminately tearing and ripping apart everything and everyone caught within reach.

With each dull thud, Nellie gasped anew. *The dreadful drum of destiny,* she thought. Each strike resonated to her very core, sickening her to the stomach. Her beloved husband, Charlie, was out there somewhere beyond—*inside*—that gloom, fighting for his country.

She came here to be nearer to him. She came here to remind herself that no matter how hard life was for her and her infant son, it was infinitely better than it was for poor Charlie. As always, she would forbid eager tears from flowing, instead returning stoically to her dingy house to continue life as best she could. Waiting. Waiting for the day Charlie returned. It pained her greatly to think that he was so close by—just a few hours away—and yet at the same time so dreadfully far.

Today, the cold had beaten her. She lingered for a moment longer, absorbing the rhythmical thudding, searching the gloom for something—*anything* upon which to fix her gaze. But there was nothing but grey.

Alfred began to stir, his tiny blue eyes opening, reacting to the stark winter chill. It was time to go.

Nellie closed her eyes, uttered a short prayer and began her descent. Just a few feet away from the precarious cliff edge and removed from the incessant wind, the temperature seemed to lift by a few degrees. Nellie leant over the pram; Alfred had closed his eyes and returned to sleep.

She pushed on further down the hill until she reached a small copse of trees and hedgerow. In the murk of the late-afternoon light, Nellie reached up and snapped off a piece of holly covered in leaves and bright red berries. She laid it gently at Alfred's feet, alongside a long sliver of ivy she had removed from the side of a stone wall on the climb up.

Crouching down, Nellie carefully parted a curtain of holly, revealing the simple snare trap that she had set yesterday. She smiled. A plump dead rabbit, its neck snapped in the wire loop, lay waiting for her. She carefully loosened the wire, removed the rabbit and reset the snare. Nellie tied a band of string around the rabbit's hind legs and slung it from the side of the pram. *The house will not go hungry for the next few days*, she thought to herself, as she continued on down towards the town.

Nellie pushed the door tightly closed and ran the brass bolt into place. She shivered, grateful to be finally home. She shared the narrow Victorian house with two other women, Dorothy and Gwen, and their children: women whose khaki men were out there fighting.

She carried the ivy and holly sprigs up to her bedroom then returned for Alfred. She clutched him carefully in her arms and made her way up the bare-boarded stairs. Her room was on the first floor and faced the front street. Before he had left for war, Charlie had done his best to liven up the drab room, whitewashing the walls and finding the money from somewhere with which to buy material for some curtains to try and keep out the weather that the old sash windows could not. A double bed, cot, chest of drawers and a writing bureau filled the space. On the floor was an old woollen rug, whose best days were long since past.

Nellie laid Alfred down in the cot and kissed his forehead.

Taking the sprigs of ivy and holly over to the empty hearth, Nellie arranged them on the fireplace, carefully removing a run of postcards that Charlie had sent from the front line.

She took the most recent one and held it to her nose, trying to distinguish the various scents held within it. One of the smells, now fading, was of Charlie himself. A musty, manly smell—not at all unpleasant—that was unique to him. On the front of the card was a picture of a solider examining the bayonet of his rifle, whilst in the top

20

right corner a pretty young woman gazed dreamily heavenwards. Charlie had hand-tinted the khaki uniform and given the lady a vivid pink dress. On the reverse of the card was her address, franked with two stamps *Passed by censor, No.443* and *Field Post Office, 14 Dec '14*. In the bottom right-hand corner, Charlie had drawn a small orange lily.

Dear Nell, a card to let you know that I am quite well & keep smiling. Your last parcel arrived this morning - thank you so much, my darling. The toffee and rice have already gone and I have used one of the candles. The Oxo cubes will come in handy to improve the 'lovely' soup we are given. Darling, I do hope you and the Boy are well & managing. Please don't send any more if it is out of your means or if it leaves you both wanting. Give my regards to Gwen, Dorothy and the kids. All my love, darling, Charlie xx.

Nellie kissed the card and placed it on the writing bureau. Taking a thin white candle from the box, she placed it in a holder at the centre of the fireplace, nestled among the holly and ivy, and lit it. Nellie smiled. It wasn't much, but it would do. She picked Alfred up and angled his face so that he could see the decorations. 'Our own little Christmas, Alfie,' she whispered. 'Just the two of us, until your daddy comes home.'

Nellie sat on the edge of the bed and pulled a blanket up around her shoulders. Gently rocking Alfred, she began to sing *Silent Night* softly.

Chapter Four

22nd December 2014, Cadgwith, Cornwall, England

A hostile wind, unhindered on its relentless journey from its origins on the east coast of the Americas, pounded the tiny fishing village of Cadgwith. With it came great torrents of rain, which lashed through the grey dawning sky. To all intents and purposes, the village appeared deserted. The only evidence of life, in the form of smoke rising from the thatched roofs nestled into the hills, was quickly whipped away and eradicated by the inclement weather.

'There goes a nice walk, then,' Juliette murmured, tugging the duvet up over her ears. 'Think it's a stay-in-bed day.'

Morton sat up, leant across to the window, pulled open the curtains and gazed out to sea. Despite all that had been playing on his mind last night, he had slept surprisingly well.

The sound of the front door closing drew Morton's eyes downwards and he spotted his Uncle Jim, toggled up in a bright yellow jacket and hat, striding down towards the village. *Surely he's not going fishing on a day like this?* Morton thought. *Madness. With Uncle Jim out of the house and Juliette drifting in and out of consciousness, now might be an ideal opportunity to speak with Aunty Margaret,* he thought.

Morton swung his legs out of the bed and reached for his dressing gown to help stave off the chilly morning air. He had forgotten just how cold these old seaside places could become in the depths of winter.

Downstairs, he found Margaret in the kitchen, rather predictably kneading a heap of dough. 'Morning,' Morton said cheerfully.

'Good morning, dear!' she replied. 'Sleep well?'

Morton nodded. 'Very well, thank you.'

'There's a pot of fresh filter coffee there for you, if you want it. Help yourself.'

'Perfect,' Morton said, pouring himself a generous cup. 'Bit rough out there today, isn't it?'

Margaret chuckled. 'Yeah, I suppose it is. You get used to it here, though. One minute it's beautiful, the next it's pouring down. I don't pay it much attention, just get on with life.'

A good philosophy, Morton thought. But did such a carefree attitude mean that big serious topics were also ignored? he wondered, glancing across the table at her. She was already dressed, wearing an optimistically flowery dress, over which she wore a white cardigan and her ever-present apron. Her hair was, as always first thing in the morning, up in tight multi-coloured rollers.

'Still up for a cliff-top walk today?' Margaret asked.

Morton nodded. 'Sounds great to me. I'm not sure you'll get Juliette out of bed, though, in this weather.'

Margaret stopped pummelling the dough and looked Morton in the eyes. 'Think it'll be a good opportunity for us to discuss our situation, wouldn't you say?'

Morton was stunned, though he probably shouldn't have been. It was exactly the way his father would have dealt with the problem—to ignore it for as long as possible then suddenly Jack-in-the-box it out into the open. 'Er…yes. Yes,' Morton finally answered. 'That would be good.'

'I mean, *if* you wanted to talk about it. I presumed that was part of the reason you wanted to come down here?'

Inexplicably, Morton flushed a deep crimson and felt his voice box tighten. Then he remembered Juliette's words about taking a step back and treating the situation as though he were investigating a genealogical case. His confidence returned. 'Yes, I would like that a lot.'

'Good, that's sorted then. We'll have breakfast, then head out.'

Morton smiled, took a sip from his coffee and sat down in front of the simmering open fire. As he stared out at the huge waves crashing into the rocky cliffs beyond the cove, he considered what was about to happen. He was about to address the most significant aspect of his past head-on. He thought of some of his past clients and suddenly fully appreciated how they had felt when he had revealed their family history to them.

Morton pulled open the front door and was greeted by a freezing blast of salty wind, laced with rain that felt like icy needles stabbing him in the face. Under normal circumstances, Morton would have either resolutely stayed indoors, or run as fast as he could to his car but he knew that he needed to have this walk and conversation with his Aunty Margaret. She stepped out as if it were a full summer's day, seemingly oblivious to the fact that they could barely stand up without being pushed and buffeted by the wind.

'Right, come on, then!' Margaret said loudly, closing the front door behind her.

Morton looked up at the bedroom window and saw Juliette, hair squally and wild, peeping out from under the duvet. She managed a vague gesture of a wave before disappearing back into bed. It had taken no work whatsoever for Morton to persuade her not to come on the walk. She had cut his apologetic explanation short and told him that under no circumstances was she going for a cliff-top walk today. And that was that.

Margaret led the way up the hill, away from the village. They passed the two neighbouring properties, one of which, Morton noted with interest, was named 'Man-o-War Cottage', then the path dwindled down to a single track so that they were forced to walk in single-file. *Not an ideal start for a momentous heart-to-heart,* Morton thought.

The path quickly reached an apex but rather than continuing round on the path, Margaret veered off beside what looked like a very tiny cottage, stone-built with a slate roof and tall chimney.

'What's this?' Morton called after her.

She turned around and said, 'An old coastguard's place. I just brought you along here for the view. Not that great today, but on a nice day...'

Morton followed her to a low stone wall and stared out. Even on a rough day like today, it was beautiful. Tucked cosily around to the right was the village, quiet and undisturbed, as if it were a miniature model set. Out from the cove rose a rocky, grass-topped headland, and then around to the left was nothing but an expansive tumultuous ocean.

'That'll clear your pipes,' Margaret remarked with a grin, drawing in huge lungfuls of air.

Morton mimicked her and enjoyed the sensation of the chilly air inside him.

'Spectacular at sunrise and sunset,' Margaret yelled.

'I can imagine,' Morton replied. He had to bring Juliette here—ideally in better weather.

'Ready to continue?' Margaret asked. 'This coastal path runs around the entire Lizard Peninsular.'

'Ready when you are.'

They continued along the narrow path in silence, each of them engrossed in their own thoughts. They crossed a stile and stepped down into a wide grassy field. Margaret slowed her pace so that Morton drew level with her, then she threaded her arm through his.

Morton smiled. *This is it.*

'So, your dad finally told you that I'm your *biological* mother, then?' she ventured. There was an unusual seriousness to her tone and she placed a stress on the word *biological*.

'Yeah, last year when he was in hospital at death's door. He didn't want to tell me, I practically had—'

'You don't have to apologise or justify it, Morton,' she interrupted, 'I would have wanted to know if I'd been you. Crikey, I'm surprised you didn't want to find out sooner.'

'Well, I did—he just wouldn't tell me,' Morton said with a wry smile.

'That's my brother for you. It's silly really; I always knew the truth would out in the end. When I was a girl, your mum and dad promised me that you'd never be told and at the time, that was the way I wanted it. Then your mum passed away and your dad told you that you were adopted—I was livid with him. We didn't actually speak for quite a while. I just thought he was teasing you by only telling you the half of it. At that moment, though, I knew you'd eventually find out everything. I even prepared myself for what I would say to you, if he had died last year when he had all that heart trouble.'

'And what was that?' Morton asked, intrigued to know how she would have handled the situation had the ball been in her court.

Margaret took a deep breath. 'I was going to sit you down and just tell it to you straight, but that nothing had changed. Your mum was still your mum and I'm still your old Aunty Margaret. You must know in your line of work that it takes more than a set of forty-six chromosomes to turn a baby into a man. I know you've had your differences with your dad, but he and your mum did a fantastic job raising you.'

'I know,' Morton agreed. As difficult as parts of his life had been, he *did* know that; they had been good parents to him. It just was not, and could not be the same as if they had been his biological mother and father.

Margaret exhaled noisily. 'As hard as it was for me to give you up, I couldn't have given you the life they gave you. I know the way society viewed such things had moved on a bit by then, but it still wasn't the done thing for a sixteen-year-old girl to raise a baby—with or without the father.'

Morton thought of his biological father and instantly felt sickened, and yet he couldn't stop his mind from wondering about the man. *What did he look like? Where did he come from? Did he have any qualities that*

25

made him a human being? Of course, they were questions that he might have to take to the grave, never knowing the answers.

The pair walked, arm in arm, through the field, the only sounds being the incessant wind and rain rustling and creaking through the hedgerows.

'Is the fact that you live down here, so far away from the rest of the family, anything to do with me?' Morton asked.

'At the beginning, yes. I won't lie—I wanted a fresh start, to be away from the family and reminders of the past. And to escape my dad—he never forgave me for getting pregnant.'

'But it wasn't your fault,' Morton responded.

Margaret shrugged. 'He was a Victorian,' she answered flatly.

Morton glanced sideways. 'He was born in 1914, though.'

'His attitudes stemmed from fifty years before that. That's probably not very fair—he just struggled raising two children by himself after my mum died.'

'That must have been difficult for everyone,' Morton said, only having a vague notion that his grandmother had died soon after giving birth to Margaret. His grandfather's apparent aloofness went some way to explaining his own father's distance towards his children.

'It wasn't easy, let's just say that. Anyway, to answer your question fully, I did want to escape the past and so came down to Cornwall as a teenager and found a life here. Met Jim, married him, had the girls and here I shall be buried.'

'Fair enough,' Morton said.

'I often wonder if things might have been different if my mum had been alive when I was pregnant.'

A long pause followed, as they both considered the different paths their lives might have taken had Margaret's mother survived childbirth.

It was Morton who finally broke the silence. 'Could you tell me about my birth?'

Margaret smiled and glanced out to sea. She took her time to answer. 'As soon as I began to show, I was parcelled off from our house in Folkestone to my granny's house—you know, Nellie— Charles's wife. She was in her eighties by then but still in good health. She had a lovely cottage outside Canterbury and I stayed there with her for several weeks. Funnily enough, she was the one who taught me how to bake. Wonderful cook she was, too. If I could get my fruitcake or wholemeal bread half as good as hers, I'd be happy. She taught me about birds, animals and plants—the garden here looks a lot like her

26

garden did back then. I loved it there. The best thing, though, was how she treated me. She really brought me out of myself. We didn't spend much time discussing the baby and she'd talk about everything as 'before the event' or 'after the event'. Don't get me wrong, she wasn't being judgemental or anything. She was a fine woman, was Granny.'

'Did she ever talk about Charles?' Morton asked, aware that he was allowing the conversation to stray slightly off-topic.

Margaret shook her head. 'Not that I can recall. I suppose it was so long ago, wasn't it? He'd been dead what…well, it was exactly sixty years. Even her second husband, Len had died by then.'

'So then what happened?'

'Then *the event* happened. Granny called for the village midwife, Mrs Blake, who turned up on an old three-wheeled bicycle and helped me to deliver upstairs in my bedroom. *The event* was over, Mrs Blake left and Granny took the baby and put it—sorry, you, away into another room and called your father. A few hours later he and your mum arrived to collect you.'

'That must have been hard for you,' Morton said, almost inaudible against the noise of the wind.

'Yes, it was. It really was. But there I was being told by everyone that it would be in your best interests to be looked after by Peter and Maureen.' She paused. 'It was only when I had my own children that I realised how right they were—I was in no position to give you a life. Fortunately life gave me another chance with Jess and Danielle.'

He didn't know why, but her last sentence cut right through him, like a cold knife. He had learnt and understood so much, and yet the inescapable truth was that she had given him up then gone on to have two further children, whom she had kept, nurtured and cherished.

Margaret sensed his unease. 'Sorry, that can't have been a very nice thing to hear. I didn't mean it how it sounded.'

'It's fine. Why shouldn't you have gone on to have children with Uncle Jim?' Morton said. He needed to move the conversation on. 'So how long did you stay on with Nellie after the birth?'

'A good few weeks. I think she needed to see that I was totally over the birth—no baby blues or that I wasn't going to do anything silly. I remember, she had a real thing for me telling her my feelings. She always wanted to know what was in my head.'

'And did you get over the birth okay?' Morton asked. 'It can't have been easy for a sixteen-year-old—especially given the circumstances of how it happened.' Morton shot a glance at Margaret to see how his

27

comment—obliquely touching at the sensitive subject of his conception—had been received. From her reaction—face flushed and clearly embarrassed—he had skated too close.

'It was fine,' she stammered, turning her head away from him.

He had pushed too far.

Margaret removed her arm from his and began fishing in her pockets, mumbling something incoherently. 'Polos,' she finally said, pulling out a packet. 'Would you like one? I always enjoy them on a walk like this,' she said cheerfully.

Morton reached out for one and thanked her. He knew that was it; any other questions, fears or worries surrounding his birth and adoption would have to wait—possibly indefinitely, for an answer. His Aunty Margaret, just like his father, had a knack of switching off a conversation like a light.

Morton took one of the multitude of free parking spaces available on Helston high street. The town—the nearest to Cadgwith—was, like the rest of Cornwall out of season, eerily quiet. Strings of lights and colourful Christmas decorations neatly laced up opposing shops along the length of the road. The wind had continued to batter the peninsula; the ominous dark clouds above looked like the current break in the rain was just going to be a short pause.

'So, how do you feel now?' Juliette asked, as she clambered out of the Mini. Their entire conversation on the drive here had been dominated by Morton recounting his morning walk with Margaret.

'I don't know really,' he replied, taking her hand in his. 'It's weird. On the one hand, it addresses gaps that my brain has questioned over the years, but on the other, it felt like she was talking about someone else. That baby was me...and yet it didn't feel like that. She's my mother...but not. Like I said, it's weird.'

Juliette nodded and squeezed his hand. 'I get it. Sort of. Do you think there's more to be said?'

Morton considered the question. 'It's hard to know. I feel like she's holding back on something, but owing to the way it all happened to her, I feel I can't really probe too deeply.'

'Well, I think that what you're going to have to do is to let your mind relax and when questions pop into your head, sort them out into ones you can actually ask her—like things that went on with her granny—ones that she'd be happy to answer and ones that you just can't ask at the moment. Maybe one day the time will come when she can talk about it.'

Morton nodded. 'Maybe,' he said quietly. 'Shall we go for a pasty lunch somewhere?'

Juliette laughed. 'You really are a Farrier, Morton.'

'What do you mean?'

'I mean, the way you can cut from a serious topic straight to the banal. From adoption to pasty in one fell swoop.'

Morton smiled and led them into a cosy-looking café with fake snow sprayed all over the steamed-up windows. The warmth of the place hit them instantly and they both realised then how cold they had been on their short stroll from the car.

'Table for two?' a young lad asked, attempting efficiency by speaking to them whilst twirling to grab two menus. He failed miserably and dropped them to the floor.

'Yes, please,' Juliette answered, trying to stifle a snigger.

'Sorry,' he muttered, flushing red. 'There you go. Follow me.'

They followed him over to a table in the corner of the room.

'Here we are,' the waiter said, proudly indicating a small table beside an over-dressed Christmas tree, crowned by a garish, lopsided fairy.

'What drinks can I get you?' he asked, producing a scrawny notepad and pen.

'Latte for me, please,' Morton said.

'Same for me, please,' Juliette added.

'Lovely,' the waiter mumbled, darting off.

'Aren't there laws about under-age children working in cafés?' Morton whispered across the table.

'Bless him,' she said with a smile, as she skimmed the laminated menu. 'I think I just fancy a pasty. What about you?'

'Yeah, traditional Cornish pasty will be lovely.'

The waiter returned with a tray precariously balanced on one hand, fingertips splayed underneath. As he lowered the tray to the table, it slipped, sending a slop of frothy coffee over the edge. 'Oops, sorry,' he apologised.

Morton was about to complain, but, when he looked up at his young innocent face something in him softened. He could only have been fifteen or sixteen. *A hundred years ago*, Morton thought, *you would have been exactly the sort to have answered Kitchener's call and have been sent off, gun in hand, to fight a war you knew nothing about and from which you would likely never have retuned.* 'It's fine, don't worry,' Morton reassured him. He ordered the food and watched the boy scuttle off to the kitchens.

'He's a bit incompetent,' Juliette remarked.

'Yeah, but he's young. Leave him alone. I'll still tip him at the end.'

'What's got into you, being so generous? The season of good will?'

'Just got me thinking about my great grandfather and all the other lads going off to war not much older than him.'

Juliette swept her hair back. 'Listen to you, getting all sentimental now you're finally researching your own family tree! I take it by this you're feeling more of a Farrier now?'

Morton nodded, as an excited feeling surged through him at the thought of discovering his own ancestral heritage, maybe even making contact with new living relatives.

'What have you actually found out about this Charles Farrier chap, then? Did I hear you say he was killed in the First World War?'

'Yeah, December 1914,' Morton answered, before beginning to relay the highlights of his discoveries, only stopping to accept the delivery of two large Cornish pasties.

'See, you've got a family now,' Juliette said once he had finished his recount.

Morton nodded his agreement and, when he had finished his mouthful of pasty, said, 'I'd like to do a bit more research while we're down here, so that I can show Aunty Margaret. If that's okay with you?'

'You can do more tonight, can't you? I'm happy watching TV and relaxing.'

Morton leant over and kissed her on the lips. 'I love you.'

'Love you too. Weirdo.'

A thick church pillar candle at the centre of the dining table and the low flicker from the Christmas tree lights sent obscure black shadows around the room. The final morsels of a fish pie had been consumed and the wine bottle emptied.

'Lovely dinner, thank you, dear wife,' Jim barked. 'Right! Who's coming to the Cadgwith Cove Inn, then?'

Margaret fired an uncertain look at Morton. 'I don't mind. If you'd rather stay and do a bit more research into my grandad, then that's okay, too.'

'Let's do that,' Morton said.

'I was hoping you'd say that,' Margaret said with a laugh.

'I'll join you, Uncle Jim,' Juliette replied, standing from the table.

'That's the spirit!' Jim roared.

'Just you watch yourself, James,' Margaret joked. 'Juliette—please feel free to arrest him, if he misbehaves.'

'Will do,' Juliette said, playing along.

Jim and Juliette pulled on their shoes and coats, then disappeared down to the pub.

'Let's get on with it, then,' Morton said enthusiastically, placing his laptop on the dining table.

Margaret rubbed her hands with glee and perched down beside him. 'What's first?'

'Well, I'm going to see if his regiment's unit diaries are online. Some are, some aren't—bit of pot luck, really. They don't usually mention names in them, but it will be good to see what he was up to and what happened in the unit the day he died.'

'Oh, yes!' Margaret said avidly.

Morton opened up the National Archives website and navigated to the unit war diaries, series WO 95. He typed *Royal Sussex Regiment* into the search box. 'Bingo!' he said. 'Second Battalion unit diaries available for the grand sum of three pounds thirty, which includes five hundred and eighty-one files covering August 1914 to April 1919! That'll keep us busy.'

'Crikey. What happens now?'

'I buy them then download them,' he responded with a smile, as he fumbled in his pockets for his credit cards.

Margaret shook her head in amazement, as Morton completed the transaction. Moments later, the four downloaded files comprising the entire Battalion's First World War history appeared onscreen.

'Right, let's start at the beginning, then.' Morton opened the first file. The opening page, scanned in high-resolution colour, was wrapping-paper-brown with the simple typed words *2nd Battalion Royal Sussex Regiment Aug - Dec 1914*. His great grandfather's war movements could be plotted within those one hundred and seventy-two pages. Somewhere in there, among the death and destruction, was whatever had happened to end Charles Ernest Farrier's life.

Morton scrolled down until he was greeted with the very first pages of Army Form C. 2118. The page was divided into three typed sections: *Hour, Date, Place* in the left-hand column, *Summary of Events and Information* in the centre and *Remarks and references to Appendices* on the right. Hand-written on the page in a purple scrawl were the initial preparations of the Battalion in Woking, England in August 1914.

'Do you want me to read *everything*?' Morton asked. 'There's quite a lot here.'

'Oh yes, even if it takes all night!'

'Okay,' Morton began, clearing his throat. 'Here we go, then.'

It took time for Morton to initially decipher the particular scrawl of the Battalion commander, but once he had adjusted to the peculiarities of his handwriting, he was able to read quickly through the diaries, only stopping to make his own notes or to answer queries from Margaret.

'So, Charles took part in the First Battle of the Marne and the First Battle of the Aisne,' Morton muttered, as much to himself as to Margaret. 'He survived all that but didn't survive the year, just like most of the original regular soldiers. The British Expeditionary Force was all but wiped out by the end of 1914, awaiting fresh blood. Sad. Very sad.'

'Gosh, what an awful time for him,' Margaret lamented once they had reached December 1914. She sighed and tried to stifle a yawn. 'Sorry!'

'No, it's getting a bit tiring now,' Morton said, stretching out. 'Shall we have a break?'

'We could do and I could put the kettle on. Or, a better idea: why don't you just read what he was doing exactly one hundred years ago today, then maybe read the next entry tomorrow?'

Morton smiled. It wasn't exactly his usual style of genealogical investigation, but he could see how delighted Margaret was with her suggestion. 'Yeah, that's a lovely idea. Hang on then.' He returned his focus to the laptop screen. '22nd December 1914. We relieved the Seaforths commencing at 7.30am but did not actually finish the relief until 3.20pm. The chief cause of which was the appalling state of the communication trench. During the time we were relieving, the enemy collected in large numbers behind the houses in the orchard and attacked the Lancs, succeeding in bombing them out of their trenches. This line had to be dug during the night 22nd/23rd. Some of the Germans got into the left of our fire trench and the left of our support trench. We constructed barriers and bombed each other vigorously. The fire trench on the right of our line was exceedingly wet, one half of the company had to stand waist deep in water until we were relieved on the 23rd by the Grenadier Guards. Lieutenant Williams and one rank and file killed.'

Morton exhaled slowly as he considered the words he had just read. Just like all the other entries which detailed what must have been awful circumstances for the men involved, it was written in such a blasé, detached way as to render him speechless.

'Makes you wonder how on earth *anyone* survived...' Margaret uttered. 'I mean, you can't imagine just standing in a wet, muddy trench all night having previously been bombed and seeing your comrades killed day after day.'

'Awful,' Morton said. 'Just awful.'

'I'm kind of glad we're not reading anymore tonight.'

'Me too,' Morton agreed.

'Shall we have a cuppa?' Margaret suggested.

'Or we could go down the pub and join Uncle Jim and Juliette for a quick nightcap?' Morton said with a grin.

Margaret nodded. 'Let's go.'

Chapter Five

22ⁿᵈ December 1914, Le Touret, France

The company sang, without conviction, banal repetitive songs that spoke of home and of victory, as they marched wearily like a long column of ants. Charles Farrier was not singing. The greatcoat on his back seemed to be getting heavier with every new drop of rain. It felt as though for every mile he had marched, another concrete block had been added to his load. They had marched roadside from their comfortable billets in Le Touret, heading to the front, passing medical facilities, gun lines, storage depots and shelled deserted homes, whose occupants had long since fled. During the last mile, war traffic in both directions had increased substantially, with motorbuses and horse-drawn carriages busy parcelling soldiers to and from the front.

Charles raised his nose into the air; there was a definite smell lingering, which was particular to an entrenched war zone: it was the smell of mud, death and decay.

Glancing at a row of shattered wagons and horses in various states of decomposition, Charles failed to hear the large motorbus roaring behind him. A sudden wave of grey water sprayed over Charles's puttees and boots. He looked up angrily and went to shout out, but then he saw those being transported in the bus: men in shredded khaki with various parts of their bodies and souls left behind in the trenches. Men who stared out, unblinking into the abyss, unable to articulate their individual horror.

Charles returned his focus to watching the footfall of the man in front, trying to dismiss every other thought from his mind; but it was impossible. In just four months, he had witnessed and endured so much.

After being shelled heavily outside Ypres, the Battalion had been ordered to move on and help restore the line at Zandvoorde. However, disaster had struck when their Commanding Officer, Lieutenant Colonel Roland, had taken a short cut across open countryside, causing the horse upon which he rode to bolt towards the heavy fire. The Commanding Officer had been killed instantly. The Battalion had forged ahead, soon occupying frontline trenches, directly battling against heavy German artillery and gunfire.

Charles recalled with consternation what had happened next and how he was lucky to have survived. When Battalion scouts had discovered that German troops, armed with heavy machine guns, had occupied a section of nearby trench and part of Château Wood, the Battalion had been divided to attack the enemy. Charles and the rest of 'A', 'B' and 'C' companies had been ordered to advance across open country towards the German positions in the wood, whilst 'D' company attacked the trenches. Part way across the field, the Germans had opened fire and Charles had watched with renewed horror, as his friends and comrades had been cut down in front of him. The cries, the pleas for help and the anguished yelling of men realising that their life was about to come to an abrupt end had risen into the trees, merging with gunfire, explosions and German voices: a cacophony of violent death and despair. The Battalion had been ordered into yet another retreat. Charles had survived. Fifty-six men from the Battalion had not.

The singing began to fade and the men in front of Charles seemed to react to something. He looked up and realised that they had reached the opening of the first sinuous communication trench.

Charles drew in a sharp breath and felt his chest tighten. 'Here we go, then,' he muttered.

'Let's do it!' Len remarked, sharing in the jaunty *joie de vivre* that was oft rehearsed at the front, but increasingly rarely believed.

The mouth of the communication trench drew them inside, one by one. Their songs were over. Their voices were silenced. Their pace slowed.

Narrow and curved, the trench had suffered badly from the inclement weather. The floor was one thick, solid carpet of mud that reached out for each soldier's feet, sucking them down, unwilling to release its grip.

'Come on, we haven't got all day,' shouted Buggler at the entrance of the trench.

In front of him, soldiers bit their tongues as they physically picked up their feet from the consuming trench base, their progress to the front being made one slow step at a time.

Charles turned to speak to Jones, his friend from 'B' Company, who was directly behind him, but the mud refused to allow his foot to swivel, sending Charles sliding forwards. 'Damn this bloody place,' he cursed under his breath, as he corrected himself and rubbed his hands down the sides of his greatcoat.

'I beg your pardon, Farrier?' Buggler barked. 'Is there a problem here?'

'No, nothing, sir,' Charles replied.

Slowly and painfully across eight long hours, the Seaforth Highlanders dragged themselves out of the front line and the Second Battalion dragged themselves in, with the various companies being distributed throughout the trench system.

With a deep satisfaction evident on his lopsided grin, Buggler directed Charles and the rest of 'A' Company to the right-hand side of the fire trench; the part which was severely flooded.

The men silently obeyed their orders, shuffling themselves ever deeper into the foetid water, their rifles raised, surrender-like, high above their heads.

Charles felt each layer of clothing progressively and quickly yielding to the invading, freezing water; he wore no garment capable of holding it back.

The company were ordered to stand, rifles bayoneted and ready at the fire trench until they could be relieved. A day of pumping and shovelling around the clock had done little to improve the situation.

Darkness seemed to descend rapidly, as if it had fallen with the pervasive rain that continually fed the stagnant water in the trench.

Charles Farrier stood shivering. The water had reached his groin and was continuing to rise. Unable and unwilling to talk to his unseen comrades in the fire bay, he simply stared ahead and prayed that relief would come soon.

Suddenly, from somewhere over to his left, a barrage of rifle fire and muted shouts filled the night sky. The men in Charles's bay looked out in the direction of the noise, but could see nothing.

Some time later, the men were roused from whatever state of cocooned silence they had managed to get themselves into when a loud explosion ripped open the trench less than a hundred yards away.

Charles listened as rifle fire erupted, almost masking the blood-curdling screams of injured men, which rose violently into the sky.

Within minutes, the unmistakable crack of return artillery fire from the Allied trenches resounded in the air, exploding seconds later, ripping callously through mud, wood, wire and flesh.

'Sounds like Fritz is in for a pummelling tonight,' Leonard said with a feeble laugh.

Agreement came from several half-hearted laughs in the fire bay.

36

'Yes, but it sounded like we took a pummelling, too,' Charles said solemnly.

If any replies were forthcoming, then they were drowned out by the deafening roar of multiple rounds of artillery fire from both sides.

A waft of cordite drifted across the trench, an odious echo from the relentless pounding that each trench was receiving.

'There'll be more casualties tonight, yet,' Charles muttered to himself, suddenly grateful to be standing waist-deep in freezing, muddy water.

Chapter Six

Morton couldn't sleep. It was the vicious combination of too much alcohol the night before and his mind being besieged jointly by thoughts of his birth and thoughts of his great grandfather's untimely death in the First World War. He leant across to his mobile and checked the time: Five forty-eight. Despite being desperate for sleep, he knew that it wouldn't come now. He also knew that his Aunty Margaret would right now be downstairs baking some cake or other. It seemed to be a Farrier trait to get up at the crack of dawn come hell or high water; a trait he desperately hoped wouldn't be locked away in his genes, dormant and waiting to be ignited.

Morton swung his legs out of bed and, in the near-blackness of the bedroom, fumbled about for his slippers and dressing gown. He deftly stole from the room, gently closing the door behind him.

Downstairs, as expected, he found Margaret with a smudge of flour across her face, and up to her arms in cake mixture.

'Morning—a bit early for you, isn't it?' Margaret greeted.

'Morning, Aunty Margaret,' he replied, waiting for his tired brain to wake up before more conversation could happen. 'Too early.'

'Nonsense. Best part of the day.'

Morton took a seat at the kitchen table and flaked dramatically onto his arms. 'That's what Dad would say,' he mumbled.

'Come on, now, Morton. Fix yourself a coffee and get on with some research!' Margaret said playfully.

Morton groaned, although the idea appealed to him. *It's a good time to take advantage of Juliette being asleep,* he reasoned.

'I've dug out my old box of family papers and what-have-you— thought you might find it of interest. There's also a photo of Grandad Len in his uniform.'

Morton sat up, his interest piqued.

'It's in the lounge. Probably nothing much in there to help you with Grandad Farrier's war service, but worth having a rummage.'

Morton made himself a strong coffee and wandered into the lounge. Margaret had lit a fire some time ago, but it had yet to take the edge off the chilliness. He pulled his dressing gown tightly around him and sat down on the floor beside the plastic storage box. On the top of

38

the box rested an image of a First World War soldier. Morton picked it up and studied it carefully. It was a sepia studio portrait, printed onto a standard postcard—a common practice amongst men about to leave for the front.

The man in the photo, proud and handsome, had brown hair and a neat pencil moustache, which sat over a straight, serious mouth. There was a warm familiarity to his dark young eyes. He wore a standard khaki serge tunic with knee-length khaki puttees. Around his waist and over his shoulders was the 1908 pattern Mills Webbing equipment supporting two sets of five pouches.

Morton flipped the postcard over. On the back was handwritten, 'August 1914.' In front of it, a word or series of words had been entirely obliterated by heavy black scrawl. He held the picture up for a closer inspection and briefly considered scanning it in high resolution to try and determine the words that somebody had deemed it necessary to remove, but the thickness of the censoring was such as to make its revelation impossible.

Turning over the image in his hand, Morton stared at the face. So naïve and ignorant of what the next four years would bring him. *He was very lucky to survive unscathed for the entire duration of the war,* Morton considered.

'Did you say that Len was a prisoner of war?' Morton called into the kitchen.

'That's right. Don't know much more than that,' Margaret answered with a chuckle.

Morton considered that being a prisoner of war was probably what had saved him.

'There's a couple of postcards from him in that box,' Margaret added.

Morton set the photo down and carefully lifted the lid of the storage box. Inside, he was greeted with a random assortment of papers, and family detritus, whose discolouration testified to their age.

'Do you mind if I take photos of some of the documents?' Morton called.

'Oh, no, go ahead. No worries. I'm glad someone's taking an interest in it all—Danielle and Jess aren't really bothered.'

'Great.' With a flurry of anticipation, Morton began to work his way through the box, which ranged in content from serviettes emblazoned with Margaret and Jim's silver wedding date, to original certificates. Among the collection were Margaret's birth and marriage

39

certificates, his grandparents and Alfred and Anna's marriage and their death certificates. He studied and photographed each item, adding relevant details to his growing Farrier family tree as he progressed. From a batch of well-preserved burial board records and notices from the Poor Law Guardians in Lambeth, Morton deduced that Charles Ernest Farrier's early life in London had been blighted by extreme poverty, his parents having been taken to a pauper's grave in their early forties.

'This is a real treasure trove, Aunty Margaret,' Morton called. 'Most genealogists would kill to have these records.'

'I'm not sure why or how I ended up with them after Dad died, but there you have it.'

Morton next found an original marriage certificate for Charles Ernest Farrier and Nellie Ellingham. It was dated 14th June 1912 and took place in the Eastbourne Wesleyan Chapel. Morton wondered if Charles had ended up in Eastbourne in search of a better life outside of London. Certainly he had remained in the town, as Alfred's birth certificate confirmed it to have been his place of birth. He noted with interest that one of the witnesses to the ceremony was Leonard Sageman, who would later marry Nellie following Charles's death.

Finally, he reached the only items pertaining to the First World War: two postcards from Len to Nellie. The first was of a vignetted, beautiful woman gazing sidewards with a happy, smiling face. The postcard had been crudely hand-tinted to enliven the drab sepia. '*January 1915*,' Morton began quietly, '*My Dearest Nell, Just to let you know that I am A1 & still smiling. I am in a POW camp - Garrison Lazarette - in Münster. I've been receiving treatment following a minor skirmish—nothing to worry about. Still receiving parcels & letters here. I hope you have been able to sort out the insurances and that Charlie's will that I sent you has been officially recognised. Please write with your new address as soon as you have moved. With fond regards, Len.*'

Morton set the postcard down and picked up the next. On the front was an embroidered basket of violets with the words 'To Nell' sewn in neat purple letters at the bottom of the card. Morton flipped it over and read aloud. '*18th March 1915. My Dearest Nell, Thank you for your lovely long letter and parcel. I am happy that you have settled into your new home near Canterbury. No doubt you will be missing Gwen and Dorothy, but you will soon make new friends. I'm sure it's for the best. I am still A1 and fighting fit. I have moved to another camp - Reserve Lazarette, Bergkaserne. Good doctors. Dreadful food. Will close now. Love, Len.*'

Now fully awake, Morton jotted down the salient points from the postcards on his notepad. He was particularly intrigued by Nellie's moving near to Canterbury in 1915. He suspected that, as a widow with a young son, she was unable to continue living at her previous residence in Eastbourne. He looked at the burgeoning Farrier family tree, with the new additions of birth, marriage and death dates taken from the various certificates in his Aunty Margaret's collection. One certificate notably missing was Nellie's marriage to Leonard Sageman. He carefully double-checked the bundle of certificates, but it was definitely not there.

After carefully placing the documents back inside the box and reattaching the lid, Morton took his notepad and pen to the table and opened up his laptop to confirm Nellie and Len's date of marriage. After a quick few taps on the keyboard, the Findmypast website told him that the marriage had taken place in the March quarter of 1919 in the district of Canterbury. Luckily for him records for St Peter's Church, in which the marriage had taken place, had been scanned and entered onto the website as part of their Canterbury Collection. Seconds later a scan of the whole page, containing four original marriage entries was presented onscreen. Morton zoomed in and read the entry. They were married, by licence, on the 14th January 1919, both of them residing in the village of Westbere. Leonard's occupation was noted as 'Painter & decorator' and both the bride's and groom's fathers were listed as deceased. The ceremony was witnessed by one George Clarke and one Maisie Worboise.

Morton jotted down the entry, zoomed back out and was about to close the tab when he spotted something. The entry directly below Nellie and Len's was for the marriage of George Clarke and Maisie Worboise, who had married on the same day. Morton smiled, considering that they were likely four friends who decided to marry together. Strangely, however, Leonard and Nellie had not reciprocated being witnesses to their wedding.

'Cake! Coffee!' Margaret chanted, as she strode into the lounge with a large tray brimming with an assortment of homemade cakes and biscuits—all with a Christmas theme.

'Perfect,' Morton said. 'I could do with a break.'

With an overly dramatic tug, Margaret pulled back the thick curtains, as if unveiling a grand masterpiece. Daylight streamed into the room, a reluctant sun emerging in the sky.

'Looks like it's going to be a nice day,' Morton observed.

'Fancy a trolley into Truro? Do the touristy things like the cathedral? Have a meal out?' Margaret asked, sitting opposite him at the table.

'Lovely,' Morton said, leaning over and taking a fresh cup of coffee and a snowman shortbread. After taking a mouthful of each, he said, 'I was just finding out a bit more about Leonard. He and Nellie married in January 1919. Seems pretty quick to me.'

She raised her eyebrows and nodded. 'Why not? After all that loss and devastation, why would they wait around? After all, there was a terrible shortage of men—I think Granny probably didn't want to hang about.'

'I suppose so,' Morton agreed, having not considered the huge post-war disparity between the sexes.

'I'd say they had a long courtship via letters for several years until he was released from the POW camps at the end of the war.'

'Yeah, I guess he was incarcerated until after the Armistice,' Morton answered, returning his focus to his computer. 'I'm just going to see if there are any POW records still surviving for him. I know the International Red Cross have digitised some of their records. Let's take a look.'

Margaret carried her coffee over to the table and stood behind Morton, watching excitedly as his fingers darted around the keyboard.

'Here we go,' Morton said, indicating for Margaret to read the screen. It was a scan of a simple index card, which the International Red Cross, in their role as a go-between, had compiled.

Leonard Sageman. Soldat No. 6518 au Royal Sussex 2me Rgt. Comp. A. Disparu depuis décembre 1914.
Rép. à Mrs Nellie Farrier, Swan Cottage, Church Lane, Westbere, Canterbury, Kent.
Priv. Royal Sussex. Wound in thigh.
Communiqué famille 4/1/15.

'Am I right in saying that *disparu depuis décembre 1914* means that he had been gone since December 1914?' Margaret asked.

'Yes,' Morton replied, without turning from the screen. 'It must have been around the same time as Charles was killed. I might just take a quick look at Len's war service, before Juliette and Uncle Jim get up and we're required to do something other than sit in front of the computer doing genealogy all day.'

42

Margaret laughed. 'I'd be quite happy doing that. I love it.'

'Me too,' Morton agreed.

He returned to the First World War record set and typed in Leonard Sageman's name. He, too had a military attestation form, having joined up on the same day as Charles Farrier in 1910. Morton waited patiently until the form loaded onscreen.

Apparent age: 22 years 8 months
Height: 5 feet 8 inches
Weight: 9 stone 9 lbs
Chest measurement minimum: 27 inches
Chest measurement maximum: 30 inches
Complexion: Fresh
Eyes: Blue
Hair: Blond
Religious denomination: C of E
Distinctive marks, and marks indicating congenital peculiarities or previous disease: None

Morton read the rest of the four-page document, but nothing further was noted about Leonard having been taken prisoner of war.

'Uh-oh,' Margaret said. 'I can hear movement upstairs. Quick, read the unit diary entry for today.' Margaret made herself comfortable and listened carefully.

'One second,' Morton said, saving Len's military attestation form before navigating his way back to the downloaded unit diary. 'Okay, ready?'

'Absolutely,' Margaret said.

'23rd December. Eppinette. Relief started at 6pm and was not completed until 6am 24th December. During these last three days of action, twenty-eight rank and file killed, wounded and missing. That's it.'

Margaret looked perplexed. 'But they only just got to the front trenches.' She paused, trying to take it all in. 'So they troop the poor beggars through those awful conditions, make them stand in waist-deep water, get fired on, then marched back out again? Golly, it's no wonder the war wasn't over by Christmas.'

'Morning,' a croaky voice called from the stairs.

It was Juliette, descending slowly in her pink dressing gown and slippers, with her hair hanging down messily around her face.

'Oh, hi, Juliette—I thought it was Uncle Jim's voice,' Morton joked.

'Ha ha,' she mumbled, sitting at the armchair closest to the fire and tucking her knees up under herself. 'God, I've got such a headache.'

'We call those hangovers, in Cornwall, dear,' Margaret laughed. 'Coffee?'

Juliette made an affirmative groaning sound that sent Margaret scuttling off to the kitchen. 'Why are you up so early?' she asked Morton.

'Couldn't sleep, so I came down to do a bit of research. I've just been looking at—'

Juliette raised her hand and interjected. 'No. Not now. Can't cope.'

Morton smiled. 'Fair enough. I'm stopping, anyway,' he said, pushing shut the laptop lid. 'I think we're going to head into Truro later, if you fancy it?'

There was another groan from Juliette, but Morton couldn't tell if it was a good groan or a bad groan.

Three hours later, Morton, Juliette, Margaret and Jim were ambling slowly through the streets of Truro city centre, bustling with Christmas shoppers.

'Won't be a minute,' Juliette said, darting into Next.

He knew she would be a minute. Several minutes, in fact. Possibly even hours.

'I'll join you,' Margaret said, leaving Morton and Jim as shopping widowers, watching the crowds of people milling about with bulging bags.

'I'm really pleased you came down, you know, Morton,' Jim said after a short silence. 'I know Margaret was a bit nervous at first but I've not seen her this bouncy for a long while—ever since the girls lived at home probably. I mean, she's always a sunny sort, if you get me, but I think it's been a bit like a black cloud hanging over her that's now lifted.'

Morton met his uncle's eyes. He had rarely seen him so serious; Morton's entire recollection of him was as a jovial, animated giant who would never be drawn on life's serious issues such as religion or politics. When such topics were raised in his presence, he would make a joke and politely excuse himself. 'I'm glad we came down, too,' Morton responded. 'I can't explain properly, but I just *needed* to come. I

44

wasn't trying to replace my mum, or for Aunty Margaret to be anybody else to me other than who she always was…'

His Uncle Jim reached out and pulled Morton into a bear hug. 'You know you're always welcome here, boy,' Jim whispered.

'Thank you.'

'Yeah, it's been hard for her. I think the hardest part was carrying the lie around her whole life.'

Morton stopped people-watching and switched his attention to his Uncle Jim. 'What do you mean?'

Jim's ruddy face, already a healthy red, flushed burgundy and Morton knew there was something amiss. 'Just that she was your birth mother and not your aunty,' he stammered.

It was very clear to Morton that his Uncle Jim was lying or at best economising on the truth. 'That wasn't the lie you were referring to, though. What did you mean?'

'Nothing, I didn't mean nothing.'

'Uncle Jim, tell me!' Morton said, suddenly feeling a wobble inside his stomach. *A lie about his birth? What now? Was she* not *his biological mother after all?*

'Nothing to declare here,' Juliette said, suddenly appearing and mock-concealing a large carrier bag behind her back.

'Me neither,' Margaret said, imitating Juliette. 'What are you boys looking so serious about?'

'Nothing,' Jim answered. 'Come on, let's go and find something to eat.'

Morton stood and watched the three of them begin to move off down the street, a hollow feeling gripping and slowly tearing at his insides.

Chapter Seven

23rd December 1914, Eppinette, France

Charles was right: there had been casualties last night amongst 'C' and 'B' companies. Many dead. Another old friend from the regulars, Arthur Jarret, among their number. Arthur, a born humourist with a fund of common sense, was well-regarded among the rank and file and Charles lamented his death bitterly. The Germans had stormed their trenches, resulting in the barrage of gunfire that Charles and his comrades had heard from their watery prison. Barriers had been erected hastily, followed by each side heavily bombing the other.

Knowing that yet again he had escaped death only by chance had allowed Charles to keep something resembling his resolve last night when his mind, suffocating in loneliness, allowed in the dark whispering thoughts that questioned his very existence in this war. He, along with the rest of the company, had stood in waist-deep muddy water all night long with no relief. The men had tried singing and talking to help pass the desperately long hours but they soon found preferable the empty silence of the battlefield and their own thoughts as company. The temperature, hovering close to freezing, had anaesthetised the water holding the men in place, mercifully numbing their lower bodies.

The sun had taken many, many hours to rise and when it had, it refused to penetrate through the dense clouds sitting just above the treeline.

As Charles stood, rifle at the ready, an alarming thought recurred in his mind, whose seed had been sown back when the Battalion had taken the two hundred and fifty German soldiers prisoner, only for them to be fired upon by their own men: the inanity that such evolved sophistication and industrialisation could result in the complete and utter destruction of humanity. Borderless, nationless madness.

Charles tried to clear his mind, knowing that such thoughts were highly dangerous. Yet they persisted, waiting in the recesses of his mind, with faces—real faces: dead and forever silenced. The faces of his friends. The faces of enemies.

He recalled an attack on the evening of 1st November when, back in Château Wood, just outside Ypres, the Germans had unleashed a determined attack on the trenches held by the Second Battalion. They had fought hard and had held their position. The following day, Charles had been one of the men sent out to assess the damage. He had discovered four German bodies within the Battalion's protective wire. Something had compelled him to do what he knew he shouldn't; to look the men in their eyes and to see them—*really* see them. They had all been young, no more than eighteen years old. He had pulled out their papers and had read their names. Ernest Eucker. Kurt Fischer. Rolf Tomczyk. Hartmut Kern. Names he was certain he would remember for ever. He had thought of their parents, still blissfully unaware that their boys were lying dead with horrendous wounds and gaping holes in their bodies in a forgotten Belgian wood. Men who would likely be denied a dignified burial. Men whose flesh would be taken by animals and insects, and whose bones would be taken by the very Belgian soil on which they had fought and died.

'Souvenirs?' Stoneham had called over with a large grin on his face when he had seen Charles with their papers.

'No, not souvenirs,' Charles had responded angrily. 'Leave them be.' Charles knew that Stoneham was a scavenger of the dead, amassing a horde of war memorabilia.

Stoneham had scoffed. 'What do you think Fritz is going to want to do with this?' He lifted up Rolf Tomczyk's limp arm, aiming his watch in Charles's direction.

Charles had watched incredulously as Stoneham had bent the arm forwards, holding the watch in front of Rolf's dead face.

'Vot iz zee time?' he had said with a hollow laugh. 'Time to die!'

'Stoneham, that's enough!' Charles had shouted, knowing that he had held no authority over him. But it seemed to work; Stoneham had let the soldier's arm fall back down to his side.

'This is in pretty good condition,' Stoneham had said, turning the dead soldier's head from side to side as he examined his *Pickelhaube*.

'Stoneham!' Charles had shouted, as he watched him wrest the helmet from the dead soldier's head.

'Oh shut up. You got a thing for Fritz or something?' he said, letting the German's head fall back to the ground.

Charles had looked on in disbelief.

'Shit,' Stoneham had exclaimed.

'What now?' Charles had demanded, walking over to the protective wire where Stoneham stood. Then he had seen it. Just in front of the woods, lying as they fell, were more than a hundred dead German soldiers, their grey corpses lying twisted and distorted, like slumped marionettes denied life from a puppeteer.

The two men had stood side by side, taking in the spectacle. A sudden eerie silence had descended upon the field and woods; the only sound came from the soft inquisitive scurrying of three brown rats, excitedly exploring the fresh corpses.

Charles had turned and observed the smug look on Stoneham's face, as if he were personally responsible for every extinguished life now in front of them. Charles had searched his being and tried to find some part of him that could share in the nationalistic elation that he knew those deaths should bring, but he just hadn't been able to find it. They were soldiers, men just like him. Men desperately hoping for an end to the war.

But the horror had continued. More shelling, more death and destruction had occurred in Château Wood before the Battalion had at last, on the 15th November, been relieved from Ypres. Rest and recuperation had finally been granted at Hazebrouck for the rest of the month.

Finally, at six pm, the water-clogged arteries of the frontline trenches began to be relieved. It was several hours later when Charles Farrier was allowed to leave his post. His mind and upper body were prepared to go, but his lower body was not. As he went to leave, his legs refused to move and he fell headfirst into the freezing water. With deep, searing pain spiking into every muscle and joint in his legs and feet, Charles agonisingly lifted each leg, one in front of the other, slowly wading his way through the trench.

When at last he set foot on the clean duckboards at the base of the communication trench, he broke. Previously stifled hot tears rolled down his cheeks, unstoppable until he breathed the first breath of air outside the trenches.

The eyes of his comrades peered out from under their caps with knowing and understanding looks engraved on their faces.

Chapter Eight

15th August 1974, Westbere, Kent, England

Nellie Sageman, clutching a small posy of orange lilies freshly cut from her garden, gently pushed open the black iron gate to the burial ground directly opposite All Saints Church in the village of Westbere. It was a still, humid day; Nellie pulled a handkerchief from her sleeve and ran it across her brow, then over the nape of her neck. She had decided to make this a short visit and to get back as quickly as possible to the shaded canopy of the two elder trees at the bottom of her garden. If she felt so inclined later, she might cut down some of the elderberries for jam-making.

She had aged well and, despite being in her eighties, Nellie had the strong well-defined features of a woman ten years younger. Her hair had whitened and her skin had thinned but inside she was still the same woman as in her twenties.

The burial ground, an overspill from the churchyard, had seen the interment of deceased parishioners since the early 1890s. Just four weeks ago, Nellie had stood grieving as her husband, Leonard's, body was added to their number. Yesterday afternoon a headstone had been erected to his grave.

Nellie reached the grave and gasped. The white granite stone was exactly as ordered, but seeing her husband's name etched in stark black letters tore at her heart anew. She silently read the inscription, tracing her bony fingers over the engraving as she read. *In loving memory of Leonard Sageman, a loving husband, father and grandfather. 2nd February 1890 – 17th July 1974.*

Taking a step forwards, Nellie placed the lilies on the grave, leant in and kissed the headstone. A long, happy and adventurous chapter of her life was now closed.

She took a deep breath and left the burial ground, making her way back along the road to Swan Cottage, the home that she had lived in since 1915, when a life insurance policy had paid out following Charlie's death. She looked up at the cottage with happiness. Painted cream and covered with a scented wisteria, the cottage was where many significant events in her life had taken place: she and Leonard had married from this house; their son, Alex had been born here and, of course, it was where Leonard had finally succumbed to pneumonia.

With a smile on her face at the thought of seeing another birth here—in her lifetime—Nellie made her way inside the welcome coolness of the cottage. She collapsed into her armchair in the lounge and exhaled noisily.

A light tapping on the lounge window made Nellie sit up with a start. The particular rhythm of the tapping told her that her son was at the door. She stood up and caught herself in profile in the mirror above the fireplace. 'Goodness, look at the state of you, Nellie Sageman.' She regretted allowing herself to doze after her visit to Len's grave, having intended to have a tidy up prior to her visitor's arrival.

She pulled open the front door and smiled. In front of her was her sullen son, Alfred, and his daughter, Margaret, who cowered behind him like a terrified animal. 'Alfred,' Nellie said in plain acknowledgement. She leant across to catch a better look at Margaret. She hadn't seen her since the funeral and noticed immediately how big she had suddenly become. 'Hello, Margaret,' she greeted, extending her arms out and pulling her into a hug.

'I can't stop,' Alfred barked. 'Here's her stuff. Telephone me once it's done.'

Nellie watched, incredulous that she had raised such a brute, as he waltzed off down the path, jumped into his blue Austin Mini and was off.

Nellie reached down and picked up the leather suitcase abandoned by Alfred and looked at Margaret. She was wearing a long flowing dress, which she guessed was her son's ashamed way of trying to conceal the bump. 'You don't need to look so terrified,' Nellie whispered. 'Come on in, I bet you're stifling hot.'

Margaret silently followed Nellie inside the house.

'Take a seat,' Nellie said, gesturing to the sofa and armchairs.

Margaret sat herself down in the nearest armchair—Len's armchair—and Nellie had to stop herself from asking her to move in case he came in from the garden. *He's not coming back...* she told herself.

'Would you like a drink? Something to eat? I've been baking—fruit cake, Bakewell Tart, scones?'

Margaret shook her head, her gaze set to the floor.

Nellie clasped her hands together and made Margaret jump. 'Right, listen to me, Margaret Farrier. You're not going to spend the next few weeks here like a timid little mouse, okay? I'm not your father and I won't treat you as he has done. So, I'm going to make you a nice cup of tea and a piece of cake and when I come back, you're going to have a smile on your face and you're going to say whatever it is that's bothering you.'

And with that, Nellie strode from the room, desperately hoping that her tactic might bring Margaret out of her self-imposed shell.

Chapter Nine

24th December 2014, Cadgwith, Cornwall, England

The fire crackled noisily in the lounge, as the flames hungrily devoured great chunks of seasoned oak. Margaret, with a bowl of porridge resting on her plump stomach, sat in her armchair, close to the fire. Juliette was resting her head on Morton's shoulder on the sofa opposite. Unblinking and unthinking, he was transfixed by the flames. He had suffered another bad night's sleep and his restlessness had woken Juliette. The brief conversation yesterday with his Uncle Jim had replayed in his mind over and over again all night long, like a song stuck on repeat. The more he had thought about it, the more he had wondered if had imagined Uncle Jim's sudden embarrassed discomfort, as he had tried to back-track from what he had said. Could the lie that he had mentioned Aunty Margaret carrying with her for her whole life simply be that she was his birth mother? If he trusted his instincts on the matter, as he so often needed to when carrying out his genealogical investigations, then that was *not* the lie to which his Uncle Jim had referred. Morton had had no further opportunity to speak privately with Jim, leaving the remark niggling at the front of his mind. What had made Morton even more suspicious was Uncle Jim's definite change in demeanour following their conversation. He had sat in the restaurant yesterday afternoon barely uttering a single word and avoiding all eye contact with Morton. This morning Jim had scurried down to his fishing boat at some ungodly hour. No, Morton had not imagined it, Uncle Jim had said something that he had realised afterwards that he shouldn't have—something that his Aunty Margaret had yet to tell him.

'Come on, then,' Margaret said jovially. 'Where's today's research going to take us?'

Morton smiled. 'Are you *sure* you're not getting bored with all this?' He felt a subtle but definite nod of Juliette's head on his shoulder and inwardly smiled.

Margaret looked mortified. 'No, no. I could do this all day. I just can't believe how much there is on the internet nowadays. Amazing that you can do all this research on a computer. You must never leave your house when you're working on a case!'

'If only,' Juliette murmured. 'He'd get into less trouble.'

'There's usually more to it, thankfully,' Morton said. 'Libraries, archives, churchyards—that sort of thing. There's probably more that I can find about Charles when I get home—the records for the Royal Sussex Regiment are all held at the West Sussex Record Office in Chichester. There are still a few things I can do from here, though, don't worry.'

'Glad to hear it, too!' Margaret chuckled.

Morton stood up and headed over to his laptop and notepad, receiving a glare and groan from Juliette, who slumped into the space on the sofa which he had previously occupied.

Scribbled on his notepad were a few potential lines of enquiry that he wanted to follow up. One of the postcards from Leonard to Nellie had mentioned Charles Farrier's will. Morton knew that wills of some soldiers killed in the British armed forces between 1850 and 1986 had recently been added to the government website, so he found his way to the relevant page and typed in Charles Farrier's name and date of death. One match.

Surname: Farrier
First name: Charles
Regimental number: L/7512
Date of death: 26 December 1914

Morton clicked 'Add to Basket', paid the ten-pound fee and downloaded the small file. 'I've just located Charles's will if you want to see it,' he called over to Margaret.

She stood up, set down her porridge remnants and came scuttling over to see.

The document was headed 'Informal Will' and contained a page detailing Charles's service details and date and place of death with the official typed script: *The enclosed document dated* 25.12.14 *and signed by* Charles Ernest Farrier, *appears to have been written or executed by the person named in the margin while he was "in actual military service" within the meaning of the Wills Act, 1837, and has been recognised by the War Department as constituting a valid will.*

'Come on then!' Margret said, 'don't keep me in suspense.'

Morton scrolled down to the next page, which gave, in his own handwriting, the last will of Charles Farrier. 'In the event of my death I give the whole of my property and effects to my wife, Mrs Nellie

Farrier, 14 York Street, Eastbourne, Sussex.' At the bottom of the page Charles had signed and dated the will.

'Well, that was certainly short and sweet,' Margaret commented. 'No real surprises, are there?'

'No,' Morton said. And yet something bothered him, but he couldn't work out what. As Margaret returned to her armchair and porridge, Morton reread the will several times, but he still couldn't place the cause of his unease. It was slightly strange—but perhaps a pure coincidence—that Charles had written his will the day before he was killed, but that wasn't it. Morton was desperate to read the unit war diary for the 26th December to finally see what had happened to his great grandfather. He was sorely tempted to take a sneaky look without telling his Aunty Margaret, but thought better of it. These tentative initial researches into his family tree had been one of the best genealogical cases that he had worked on simply because they were *his* family. But what he had enjoyed the most about his research was that it was a shared venture with Aunty Margaret—something to bring them closer together and remove the veils of secrecy that had hung over their relationship all these years.

'Shall I read today's diary entry?' Morton asked.

Margaret, mouth full of porridge, nodded fervently.

'24th December, Le Hamel. Brigade relieved. Marched to Le Hamel arriving about 8.30am and billeted. Capt. Wainwright at hospital...That's it—another short one.'

Margaret looked disappointed. 'So they're out of harm's way for the moment. Goodness me, I do hope he at least had a nice Christmas Day. I couldn't bear to think of him being up to his waist in muddy water or worse.' She shook her head in dismay. 'It doesn't bear thinking about. No sign of a Christmas truce for Grandad Farrier, then?'

'We'll find out tomorrow...but no, it doesn't look like it.'

'We will indeed,' she answered, standing up and heading towards the kitchen. 'Come on then, Margaret Daynes, this won't do. You've got errands to run.'

'Anything you need help with?' Morton called.

'No, I just need to pop around the village dropping presents off and what-not. Do you two still want to come to the Christingle service tonight?'

'We'd love to,' Juliette answered, before turning to Morton. 'Right, you. The weather is kind of reasonable, so do you fancy that cliff-top

54

walk you mentioned—show me where you went with Aunty Margaret the other day? It does mean you'll have to put your computer away, though.'

Morton grinned and closed his laptop. 'What about a wander through the village? Have a nice pub lunch?'

Juliette seemed disappointed. 'I fancied seeing that amazing view.'

'We'll do it another time—later maybe,' Morton promised.

'Okay. I'll go and make myself beautiful, then.'

'You don't need to,' Morton said with a smile.

Juliette lifted her hair and let it fall messily back to her shoulders. 'Yeah,' she replied, dragging the word out as she left the room.

It was late morning when Morton and Juliette stepped outside. They had wrapped up with gloves, scarves and thick winter jackets; the sun had so far spent much of the morning cowering behind ominous-looking clouds that raced across the sky, as if they were in a desperate hurry to be somewhere else.

'God, that's chilly,' Juliette said with a shudder, threading her gloved fingers into Morton's.

'Come on, then, let's get a move on,' Morton encouraged, as he lengthened his stride.

'Alright, slow down—we're not on a march,' Juliette complained.

Morton slowed his pace and the pair continued on into the main part of the village, a single lane that descended to the beach inlet before rising again the other side. Along this short stretch was a fish shop, an arts and crafts shop, a gift shop and a restaurant, all of which relied on Cadgwith's two main sources of income: the sea and tourists. Morton stepped off the road and down onto the beach, leading them past an array of fishing detritus: lobster pots, crates, baskets and an assortment of tubs out of which spewed great bundles of tangled rope. A pair of large fishing boats were hauled up onto the shingle and a range of other, smaller sailing vessels were also moored, safely tucked up away from the inclement seas.

'Those seas are really rough,' Juliette exclaimed. 'I'm surprised your Uncle Jim wanted to go out today.'

'Hmm,' Morton mumbled, thinking that he probably knew the reason why Uncle Jim would rather brave the squally Atlantic Ocean than stay in his own home.

Juliette leant in and faced Morton. 'What?'

'What do you mean *what*?' Morton said innocently.

'That noise you just made—it's the one you use when you know something more than you're letting on,' she said, her eyes narrowing suspiciously.

'I think he's trying to stay out of my way,' Morton said.

'Why would he do that? He's been so nice and welcoming.'

'Something he said yesterday that he thinks he shouldn't have said.'

'Go on,' Juliette said.

Morton recounted the brief conversation that he had had with his Uncle Jim, trying to recall it as best he could word for word.

'I think you might be reading into it, Morton,' was Juliette's initial reaction. After a short pause, she added, 'But, if you really think there's something else there, then you probably should ask your Aunty Margaret, rather than him. *If* he did let some cat out of the bag that he shouldn't have, then he obviously feels it isn't his place to discuss it.'

'I know...It's just trying to find the right moment. We're only here for another two days and I don't want to ruin it by pushing her to talk about something that she clearly doesn't want to discuss. We had all morning walking along that cliff path the other day—she could have told me then.'

Juliette rubbed her hand up his back. 'You need to make time to ask her, then; it's important. I know what will happen if you don't: we'll go back home and you'll stew on it and work yourself up, wondering what on earth it could be. It's probably nothing, or a small detail that she forgot to say.' She kissed him on the cheek. 'Try and find a moment this evening.'

Morton nodded his agreement and hoped it would be that simple. He bent down, picked up a stone and threw it into the jaws of the sea.

Chapter Ten

24th December 1914, Le Hamel, France

Shortly after eight-thirty am, the men of the Second Battalion Royal Sussex Regiment had marched into Le Hamel and been distributed among its houses and lodgings.

The Army had requisitioned several properties in the quiet village; some the owners had left voluntarily when the fighting had drawn close, others involuntarily, ousted by the military. Charles Farrier was sharing a room with six other men from the Battalion in an old redbrick town house on Rue Vayez, which, prior to the outbreak of war, had been among the most desirable properties in the area. The six-bedroomed house, close to the church, had been stripped of its fine carpets, rugs, soft furnishings and everything that had made it a home; it was now the skeleton of its former self, sorrowfully witnessing the constant stream of battle-weary men sent to rest and recuperate within its stark walls. Each room contained just six beds and a brazier for warmth. The men in the house considered themselves fortunate; others had been billeted in lofts or barns nearby, with only straw for a bed.

Charles Farrier was sharing a bedroom with Leonard Sageman, Frank Eccles, Tom Trussler, Jimmy Ramsay and Edward Partington. Each was sitting at the end of their simple metal-framed bed, their feet firmly on the floor, their boot laces open wide. Beside each man's feet were piled two filthy, snake-like puttees. Tense glances and unspoken dread passed between the men; they were braced for what they badly desired and dreaded in equal measure: the removal of their boots and uniform.

Charles drew in a long breath, took a fleeting glance at his comrades then gripped his left boot firmly. He had intended to whip it off quickly, like a plaster, so that the pain was sharp but fleeting. However, as he began to remove it, the pain was excruciating, like every bone was being broken and every muscle ripped to shreds.

Knowing that he was being watched by five pairs of anxious eyes, Charles did his best to stifle his whimpers. He tried again but the pain was simply too unbearable.

'Do you want me to do it, Charlie?' Len asked quietly from the next bed.

Charles nodded, lay down, placed the end of his pillow in his mouth and clenched his teeth together.

With as swift a movement as he could manage, Len wrenched off the boot. Charles's body tensed and flexed like he'd been electrocuted, as he bit down onto the pillow.

Moments later, both boots were discarded on the floor and the elation and relief began to overcome the agony.

The rest of the men copied Charles and paired up to remove their boots.

Charles added his socks—stained and soaked beyond recognition—to the pile on the floor and stared at his feet. They were both grossly swollen and grey in colour. Even though the boots had been removed, painful pricks seared through the numbness of the outer layers of skin.

They were the lucky ones. They weren't dead. They weren't injured. They weren't even hospitalised. More than one hundred and fifty men from the Battalion had been admitted to the field hospital in recent days suffering rheumatism, ague and swollen feet.

Charles didn't feel lucky. The hollowness inside him was growing and growing. He tried not to think about it. He slowly sat up and stripped down to his long johns and woollen vest.

After a time the six men stood, almost mechanically, and trudged painfully out of their room, through the house to an outbuilding where a communal bathhouse had been established. There, they joined a line of men from their company, similarly stripped to their underwear. Gone were the sentimental morale-boosting songs. Gone was the gung-ho bravado. The men just gazed at the floor, torpidly waiting their turn for a hot bath. Even conversation was too much.

Charles pictured the zinc bath at home. It was stored in the kitchen, only being used in front of their bedroom fire once or twice a week. He considered, with an ironic smirk, how he had sometimes felt himself dirty enough between the usual set times to warrant an extra bath. How little that naïve man had known. He wondered, *if* he survived all of this, if he could simply go back and find that naïve man again. He doubted it. He was sure that he was forever lost, consumed inside the broken man that he was today, who had seen and been the cause of so much horror and brutality.

The air in the bedroom was clouded with the steady stream of smoke drifting up from the beds. Only Tom Trussler, occupying the bed opposite Charles, had been a smoker prior to the outbreak of war. It was a habit acquired by the rest to relieve the boredom and monotony as much as anything else.

Each man was engrossed in his attempt at detaching himself from the realities of the trenches: Tom was asleep, a gentle purring sporadically rising from his pillow; Leonard was reading; Jimmy and Edward were playing cards and smoking; Frank was eating and Charles was lying down clutching the photo of Nellie and Alfred inches from his face.

'Anyone coming to the red lamps?' Frank asked, suddenly rising from his bed.

'Where are your morals?' Leonard asked, lifting his head from his book. His smile revealed the lack of seriousness to his question.

Frank shrugged. 'Lost. Last seen somewhere in Château Wood, I guess,' he answered.

'I'll come,' Jimmy responded, jumping up and throwing his cards down onto the bed.

'Charlie?' Frank asked. 'You must be missing your wife by now.'

Charles shook his head. Any moral condemnation he might have felt six months ago had long since diminished; any vice or illicit comfort a man could get to help him see the next day was fine by him. He missed Nellie terribly, and even though most visitors to the red lamps were married men, he couldn't bring himself to betray his wife. 'Not for me, thanks.'

Frank and Jimmy strolled from the room, as quickly as their aching feet could take them.

'Kitchener wasted his time putting that little pearl of wisdom in our first wartime pay-packets,' Edward said. '*In this new experience, you may find temptations both in wine and women!*'

'You must entirely resist both,' Leonard responded with a chuckle.

Edward unscrewed his canteen and raised it into the air. 'Cheers, Kitchener!' He took a swig and sighed.

'Oh, Nellie,' Charles breathed almost inaudibly, as he stared at the photo. Right now, he would do anything—anything at all—to get back home and hold her in his arms. That was all he wanted: just to hold her and stroke her face. He was worried about her, too. Edward had been sent a copy of the *Daily Mail* from 17th December, the main story in which was the bombardment of Scarborough, Whitby and Hartlepool. That German ships could just sail unhindered through the North Sea terrified him when Eastbourne was so close to mainland Europe. At

59

any moment they could cross the English Channel and attack the seaside town.

'Ho ho ho!' a sudden yell came at the door.

The men turned eagerly to see Davis from 'B' Company struggling to drag a full hessian sack into the bedroom. Quickly, he distributed letters and parcels among the men. 'Enjoy!' were his parting words.

The four men delved into their post, desperately grateful to have heard from home the day before Christmas.

Charles received a parcel and letter from Nellie. He carefully tore into the letter and read. *My Dear Charlie, Thank you for your letter 14/12/14. I'm pleased that the items were of use—of course it is not too much trouble to send them. Little Alfie and I are doing well. He grows every day, becoming more and more like you. His smile and laughter is enough to melt the hardest of souls. We muddle along, each day much the same as the last, eagerly awaiting news from the front. Dorothy and Gwen send their regards—we are a great team, the three of us—sharing the housework and employing various ingenious methods (which I daren't tell you about) to procure food for the table. Our greatest strength, though, is in the support we provide each other. Individually we are like fretful, jumpy lunatics, bouncing between good news and no news. I know I shouldn't complain—what you boys are suffering is unimaginable for us left behind. This might well be the last note you receive before Christmas, so, my love, I wish you every blessing and pray we three shall be reunited again soon. My love, Nellie xx.*

Charles smiled and wiped away a pair of tears that neatly coursed down his cheeks. Setting the letter to one side, he set about opening the parcel, taking his time and savouring the anticipation of its contents. It could be entirely empty and he'd be happy in the knowledge that his wife had sent it. Inside, he found two Christmas presents wrapped in brown paper, a bundle of candles, coffee, cherry brandy, two packets of cigarettes and a jar of homemade marmalade.

'Anything nice?' Leonard asked.

'Want to help me with this?' Charles responded, holding up the cherry brandy. He could see on Leonard's bed the summary of his post: a Christmas card containing few words. Charles shared most things with Leonard, knowing that his only contact from home was an elderly aunt who seldom wrote and never sent parcels.

Leonard smiled. 'With pleasure.'

For the six men in the shared bedroom, and for the rest of the company, Christmas Eve ended with smoking, drinking, eating and playing cards.

Charles fell asleep that night clutching Nellie's letter in his hand, warmed by the liqueur laced with the taste of the weald's summer orchard.

Chapter Eleven

19th August 1974, Westbere, Kent, England

Nellie stood at her kitchen window, watching the abundance of birdlife drawn to her garden. Flitting, dancing and fluttering, they greedily scoffed the crumbs and scraps which she had left out for them earlier that morning. A gentle breeze drifted in through the open French doors, bringing with it the chattering happiness from the birds, mingling in the air with the quiet musical offerings from her radio.

Nellie took a sip of her tea and wondered what the day would bring. She had wanted to stick to her usual routines, but her granddaughter's arrival had dictated otherwise. After four days, Nellie had yet to penetrate through Margaret's tough near-silent exterior. She sympathised with the poor girl; even today with more enlightened liberal views about the world, she was still being judged by the clinging fog of Victorian attitudes. Her son, Alfred's, disgust at her condition was evident from the very moment that he had telephoned her, asking her to see Margaret through the latter stages of her pregnancy. 'People are talking,' Alfred had said rather vaguely. When Nellie had pushed, he had elaborated further: church people, neighbours, friends and his colleagues at work. It seemed to Nellie that everyone had an opinion on the poor girl. Of course, Nellie had accepted the request only too willingly. Len's death last month had hit her hard—much harder than she would ever have envisaged—and she was certain that Alfred saw foisting Margaret on her as a solution to the double-headed problem of a grieving mother and a pregnant daughter. Although Nellie saw through his thinly veiled plan, she actually hoped that he was right, that they would become each other's support.

A sound behind Nellie made her turn and jump with fright. 'Oh goodness, Margaret!' Nellie cried. 'How long have you been standing there?'

Margaret, leaning casually against the worktop, shrugged.

Nellie swallowed down her annoyance. 'Did you sleep well?'

Margaret nodded.

'Kindly look at me when I'm talking to you, Margaret,' Nellie reproached. Her patience with Margaret's moroseness was wearing thin.

Margaret looked up sullenly.

'Listen, my girl,' Nellie began, 'if you're going to stay here for the next couple of months until the event is over, then you need to stop this sulkiness; it's not an attractive quality in a young lady.'

Margaret's eyes began to glisten. She stood up and looked Nellie in the eyes. 'I might not stay here, anyway. I might keep the baby—it's not just Dad's decision, you know.'

Nellie emitted a scoffing laugh and instantly regretted it. 'Sorry, but how are you going to cope raising a child by yourself? You're sixteen, for goodness' sake.'

'I could get myself a flat somewhere and get a job,' Margaret said without much conviction. 'What can my brother give it that I can't?'

'Your brother and his wife have a house. He has a job and money. It's a fantasy, Margaret—you'd never cope with a child by yourself.'

'How do you know what I could cope with?' Margaret demanded.

Nellie paused for a moment and lowered her voice. 'Because I've been there. I raised your father for four years by myself and it was awful. Truly awful.'

Margaret ground her back teeth, as she considered what Nellie had just said. 'But you *did* cope,' she said indignantly. 'And so could I.'

'Until I got an insurance payout following Charlie's death, do you know how I coped?' Nellie asked. Without waiting for answer, she continued, 'I coped by killing wild animals, by growing my own food, by begging and borrowing, by earning a pittance in a God-forsaken war factory; it is *not* a time I would have wished on my worst enemy.'

Margaret suddenly broke down in noisy sobs. 'I don't want the baby, anyway—not without a father.'

Nellie pulled Margaret into a long embrace. 'It's okay, we'll get through this together.'

Chapter Twelve

Morton and Juliette woke with a start. His phone, vibrating and dancing on the bedside table, was sending its shrill alarm cry into the room.

'Christ, what the hell's that on for?' Juliette demanded. 'Turn it off! It's Christmas Day and you've probably just woken half of Cornwall with that thing.'

In the darkness of the room, Morton pulled an apologetic face. 'Sorry. Happy Christmas,' he said, leaning over and kissing her.

Juliette sighed and replied drearily. 'Happy Christmas.' She flaked back down into the bed and tugged the duvet over her head. 'Night.'

Morton stepped out of bed, pulled the duvet back and switched on the bedside lamp. 'Time to get up! I've got something to show you.'

Juliette groaned. 'What is it?'

'Get dressed,' he instructed.

She looked at him incredulously. 'Really? It can't wait for another couple of hours?'

Morton shook his head and began pulling on his clothes.

With a slight huff, Juliette climbed out of bed and got dressed.

'You'll need a coat, scarf and gloves,' Morton warned once they'd crept downstairs. As soon as they were fully dressed, he looked at the time on his phone and smiled. 'Right, follow me!' he said brightly, opening the front door and stepping out into the chilly dawn air.

'God, that's freezing! Are we going far?' Juliette breathed, pulling her knitted scarf up over her chin.

'Nope, not far.'

Juliette sidled up close to him and the pair walked side by side away from the house. They walked in silence until they reached the old coastguard hut not far up the hill. Morton led Juliette out to the low stone wall and put his arm around her. 'There.'

The pair stared out over the ocean, as still and flat as if it had been frozen. As if ascending from the very depths of the sea, a large, blood red sun sat on the horizon.

'Wow!' Juliette uttered. 'That's just stunning.'

'It really is,' Morton agreed. 'Now look behind you,' he said, turning Juliette back towards the village.

'Amazing,' she said, as she took in the spectacle of the picture-postcard scene of the whitewashed thatched cottages of Cadgwith bathed in an ethereal orange glow, each tiny window glistening in the sun. Juliette exhaled. 'Okay, so maybe it was worth waking me up and dragging me out into the cold for this.'

Morton smiled. 'That wasn't what I dragged you out here for.'

'What do you mean?' Juliette asked.

Morton bent down on one knee, taking her hand in his and looked into her hazel eyes. 'Juliette Meade, will you do the honour of marrying the strange forensic genealogist stooped before you?'

A wide smile erupted on her face. 'Really? Are you joking?'

'Nope,' Morton answered, fumbling around in his jeans' pocket. 'I've got a ring and everything. You might not like it—it was my grandmother's engagement ring.' He held the ring up for her approval.

'It's beautiful,' Juliette grinned.

'Great. I'm getting arthritis of the knee here; so what's your answer?'

'Yes! Absolutely, yes!'

Morton stood up and received her warm lips to his. He had done it. He had overcome the fears that had blighted his adult life, about not being able to give his surname to another person when it didn't truly belong to him. But it did belong to him; it was his to share and his to give away to someone else. Maybe even one day to pass on to his own descendants.

'Come on, then; get this ring on me!'

Morton removed the glove on her left hand and gently slid onto her finger the simple gold band with a single diamond.

Juliette inspected her hand. 'Perfect—totally perfect! And what a perfect place, too.'

'Yeah, it's not bad, is it? When I planned it, I envisaged a gentle fluttering of snow falling down, but this will do.'

Juliette smiled and kissed him again. 'I can't believe I'm going to become Mrs Juliette Farrier.'

'Another one to add to the weird Farrier family tree,' Morton commented.

'You wait—the second we get back I'm digging out all that wedding planning stuff I got this summer at the Rye Wedding Fayre.'

'Yippee!' Morton joked.

'Come on, let's get back in and tell them the good news,' Juliette said, tugging Morton's hand.

They entered Sea View to a short burst of applause from Margaret and Jim, who were standing in their dressing gowns looking dishevelled but happy. Beside them, on the dining table was a bottle of champagne and four crystal glasses.

'You knew!' Juliette said, hugging and kissing the pair.

'He sort of mentioned it the other day. Told me to keep out the way when you two were bumbling about at the crack of dawn on Christmas Day.'

'Let's get this bubbly open, then,' Jim barked, handing the bottle to Morton to open.

The cork popped out noisily and Morton filled the four glasses.

'To Morton and Juliette,' Margaret toasted.

The four glasses clinked in the air before being raised to four happy mouths.

Five hours later, Morton, Juliette, Jim and Margaret were collapsed in front of the fire, having eaten a full traditional Christmas dinner and drunk two bottles of champagne. Strewn around their feet were pieces of shredded wrapping paper and neat stacks of assorted gifts. The pile of presents under the tree had dwindled to just one, which Juliette had been particularly guarded about Morton opening until the very last. She handed it over with a wry smile.

'What is it?' Morton asked, carefully taking it from her. It was thin and lightweight, about the size of a hardback book. He looked at her through narrowed eyes, wondering what it could be.

'Come on, man, get on with it!' Jim said.

'Leave him alone, James,' Margaret said playfully.

Morton tore open the end and carefully removed a box. 'An Ancestry DNA kit!' he exclaimed.

Juliette smiled. 'You have *no* idea how hard it was to get that—it's only available in the US, but I thought you'd like it. It seemed more comprehensive than the UK tests.'

'That's brilliant—thanks!'

'It doesn't just test one line, like maternal or paternal, but your whole ethnicity,' Juliette enthused. 'Apparently it breaks it down to geographical areas, percentages of this and that. Thought it was up your street and more... appropriate for you.'

Morton glanced up at her with a smile, and as he did so he noticed a strange conspiratorial look pass between Margaret and Jim. When they saw him looking in their direction they both redirected their gaze, almost comically. *There is definitely something wrong,* Morton thought. Judging by their reaction, it was something that his taking a DNA test might reveal.

'Right, I'd better get this mess cleared up,' Margaret announced, beginning to scoop up the scattered wrapping paper. 'Then it'll be time for the next family history instalment.'

'Or, time for the pub,' Jim teased. 'They're open for a few more hours.'

'Sounds good to me,' Juliette agreed. 'Let's go.'

'Really?' Jim asked keenly.

'Really.'

'That's the spirit!' Jim said, jumping up and heading over to the front door.

'I don't know,' Margaret said, shaking her head. She deposited all the rubbish in the bin then sat back down in her armchair with a sigh. 'Don't be too long down there, you two.'

'See you shortly, fiancé,' Juliette said, planting a kiss on the top of Morton's head.

'Bye,' he replied, before taking his usual seat at the table. 'Don't be too long, fiancée.'

'I won't—*The Friary* Christmas special's on later.'

'Great,' Morton responded sarcastically, as Juliette and Jim headed through the door. *The Friary* was the last thing he wanted to see. The programme was filmed in a stately home owned by the Earl of Rothborne, who had been embroiled in Morton's last genealogical case. The future of the show hung in the balance whilst a prominent court case was being tried at the High Court, which would decide the very future ownership of the house. Much of the evidence being used against the Earl and Countess of Rothborne had been uncovered by Morton in his quest to find the whereabouts of an Edwardian housemaid. No, Morton would definitely not be watching *The Friary* Christmas special.

'Right, today's unit diary entry, then,' Morton said.

'Before you do,' Margaret began from her seat by the fire, 'come over here a minute. There's something I need to tell you.'

'Okay,' Morton said, instantly fearing the consequences of whatever it was she was about to tell him. He sat himself down in the chair opposite her and braced himself.

'You don't have to look so worried,' Margaret said.

'It's something to do with my birth, isn't it?' Morton said.

Margaret nodded solemnly. She drew in a deep breath and seemed to hold on to it for an eternity. 'It's something I wasn't going to tell you. But after seeing you these last few days doing your genealogy and seeing that DNA thing from Juliette, I think now it's something you should be told.'

'Go on,' Morton said quietly. He was trying to cancel out the panicked flurry of activity going on in his own mind, as it frantically tried to pre-empt his Aunty Margaret with whatever revelation she was about to make. But nothing in his head made any kind of sense.

Another long pause followed until she spoke, her eyes fixed to her feet. 'Not to put too fine a point on it, but the story about your conception is somewhat inaccurate.'

'What do you mean?'

'I lied about it… I wasn't…the story your father told you last year isn't true: I wasn't…attacked.' Her eyes finally met with Morton's.

'What?'

'I mean it was consensual.'

'Why did Dad tell me what he did, then?'

'He didn't know. Doesn't know.'

'Why did you lie about it?'

'Shame. Morality. Other people's attitudes—I was sixteen, remember.'

Morton felt as though he had just been kicked hard in the stomach, as his understanding of his own past took on yet another new form. For the past year and a half, he had been struggling with the inconceivable notion that his father was a rapist, that half of his DNA stemmed from a vile criminal whom he would never meet, nor would ever want to meet. But despite that stark horrible fact, questions about his father had remained, raising their ugly heads, demanding answers. *What was his name? Where did he come from? Who were his parents? Did he father other children?*

Morton refocused. Margaret was silently weeping.

'I'm sorry, Morton—I really am. I know how hard it must be to hear all this.'

He knew he should get up and comfort her, to tell her that it was okay, but he couldn't. He was fixed to the armchair, weighted down by the impact of her confession. His real biological father was a normal man. A man out there, living somewhere. 'Who was he?' he asked in a small, squashed voice.

Margaret tugged a handkerchief from her sleeve and dabbed her eyes. 'I'll tell you everything, Morton, but I warn you—what I know isn't much at all.'

Morton nodded as tears welled in his own eyes.

'His name was Jack. He was about eighteen or nineteen at the time and he was American. He was-'

'American?' Morton interjected, trying to absorb the pace of the information that he was receiving.

'Yes, American.'

'From which part?' he asked.

'I'm afraid I don't know. I've got something in my head that he might have mentioned Boston and a degree in archaeology or something. He was staying with his parents in the guesthouse next door to us in Folkestone. He was there for a few days and we got friendly. We would just sit outside chatting, wandered around town together—that kind of thing. Then on his last day he took me to the pictures and afterwards we sneaked into a pub, had a few drinks and…we got close. The next day he went back to America and I never heard from him again.' She sat back and sighed. 'He said he would write with his address, but he never did.'

'So no further contact with him?'

Margaret shook her head vehemently. 'Nothing.'

'Do you know his surname?' Morton asked softly. His father's surname. *His* surname. The one he should be giving to Juliette. He thought it ironic that just a few hours ago he had fully embraced the Farrier surname because even if he had known the identity of his father, he wouldn't have wanted to take his name. *But now this…*

Margaret shook her head again. 'No, he was just Jack.'

In just a few short minutes, Morton's whole perception of his past had shifted on its axis. For the first time in his life, he knew who his biological parents were, albeit with limited paternal knowledge. Despite the emotional depth of what he had been told, on a genealogical level, the information was scant and inadequate. 'Is there anything else?'

'No, sorry,' she answered.

'What about his appearance?'

Margaret sniffed and laughed. 'Just take a look at a photo of you at eighteen and you'll see what he looked like.'

Tears began to roll down Morton's cheeks as a visual image of his father entered his head. He looked like him and shared his interest in history.

'Listen, Morton. I know what you're going to do next and I sincerely wish you luck with it. But please, *promise* me I won't ever get to hear about it. Not anything at all.'

Morton knew to what she referred. 'I promise.'

'And I think the same should go for your father, too. It would be enough to give him another heart attack.'

The weight pinning Morton down had lifted; he crossed the room and hugged his Aunty Margaret. Reciprocal tears flowed, embodying a complex tangle of emotions that had spanned forty years.

The truth had, at last, been revealed.

After several seconds, it was Margaret who broke the embrace. She dabbed her eyes and said, becoming stoic, 'Well, this *certainly* won't do. I'd better get in that kitchen and get washing up.'

Morton couldn't help but smile at witnessing that peculiar Farrier family trait once again kicking into action. *The hit-and-run gene.* 'I'll come and dry up for you.'

'No need,' Margaret called. 'I'd rather you read the diary for today and did some more research. You're going home tomorrow—we're running out of time!'

Under normal circumstances, Morton might have persisted, but he guessed that she needed time by herself to comprehend the implications of her own confession. 'Okay,' he responded, switching on his laptop. Before he did anything else, and while it was still fresh in his mind, he created a new file entitled *Jack*. In it, he quickly typed all that he had just learnt about his biological father, which amounted to just a few short sentences. Many would have considered the limited information hopeless, but he was a forensic genealogist: he *would* find his father.

'Come on, then!' Margaret hollered from the kitchen.

'Sorry, just got distracted.' Opening the Battalion unit diary, Morton scrolled down to the correct entry. 'Here goes. 25th December, Le Hamel. In spite of the fact that at one time on the evening of 24th we were ordered to proceed at 9am Xmas day to relieve the 6th Brigade near Cambrin, we escaped, for the order was cancelled at 11.30pm on 24th. Xmas day was spent in peace, the Brigade, however, being prepared to move at an hour's notice. Princess Mary's gifts and their Majesties' Xmas cards were issued.'

'So, a peaceful Christmas for Grandad Farrier, then,' Margaret pondered from the kitchen. 'Not quite the romantic truce in No Man's

Land that I had envisaged, but at least he wasn't in the trenches. A near miss, though, by the sounds of it.'

'Are you sure I can't read the entry for the 26th already?' Morton pleaded.

'Very sure!' came the reply.

It was *really* starting to go against his genealogical grain to sit on a document that held such importance. But, wait he would. His thoughts returned to Charles Farrier's will. What was it that had bothered him about it? he wondered, reopening the document onscreen. He re-read it for the umpteenth time. It was a standard, simple last distribution of Charles's effects; the content was not the cause of Morton's unease, he realised: it was the handwriting. *But what about it?* Zooming into the document, he studied it carefully, following the neat cursive letter formations. He looked at Charles's signature at the bottom of the page. It was the letter *h*, with a fancy flourish at the tip that he felt he had seen somewhere before. *Where had he seen it?* The only documents that he had seen with Charles's handwriting on were his will and his original marriage certificate. Pulling out his phone, he opened his photographs and began to swipe through the pictures that he had taken since being here. He stopped before he reached the image of Charles's marriage certificate; something had caught his eye. It was the postcard written by Leonard to Nellie in March 1915. His splayed fingers brought the photo up close. 'This doesn't make any sense,' Morton mumbled.

'What's that?' Margaret shouted.

'Hang on,' Morton replied, frantically tapping keys on his laptop and opening vital documents. 'Oh my God.'

Margaret came scuttling out of the kitchen with a tea towel draped over her left shoulder. 'Whatever's the matter?'

'Look at this,' Morton said, sliding to one side so that Margaret had an unobstructed view of his laptop. He clicked on Leonard Sageman's 1910 military attestation form and zoomed into his signature.

'What am I looking at?' Margaret asked, squinting at the screen.

'Just look at his signature,' Morton replied.

'Right.'

'Now look at this,' Morton said, bringing up the copy of Charles and Nellie's 1912 marriage certificate. He zoomed into the bottom of the page, where the bride, groom and witnesses had signed their names.

'Yes,' Margaret said, confusion in her voice. 'The same signatures. What about it?'

'Now look at this,' Morton said, clicking on the 1919 marriage certificate of Nellie to Leonard Sageman.

'Oh!' Margaret yelped. 'Grandad Len's signature's changed completely.'

Morton turned to face her. 'Yes, it has. And you see the fancy letter *h* in Charles's name?'

'Yes.'

'Look at this.' Morton brought up the photo that he had taken of the March 1915 postcard Leonard had sent to Nellie. He moved the cursor to the word *fighting*.

'It's the same fancy *h*!' Margaret exclaimed. 'But how can that be? Surely you're not saying that they're the same person?'

Morton shook his head. 'No, definitely two separate people—they enlisted together in 1910, remember. *One* of them died on 26th December 1914 and the other was taken as a prisoner of war.'

'Sorry, I'm totally lost.'

'I think *Len* was killed on the 26th December and, for some reason, Charles took his identity and was then taken prisoner of war.'

'Why would he do that?' she asked incredulously. 'To put poor Nellie through all that grief?'

Morton shrugged. 'She must have known fairly soon after being told that Charles was dead that he wasn't at all. Those postcards you've got, supposedly written by Len are clearly from Charles—she would have spotted that straight away. He hasn't really made much effort to disguise his handwriting, has he?'

'My goodness,' Margaret said, sitting beside Morton. 'What a shock! Are you really sure about all this?'

'There's more evidence, yet.'

'Oh, golly—go on.'

Morton pulled up the scratched, sepia portrait of Leonard Sageman in his military uniform taken in August 1914. Beside it, he placed the physical description of Leonard on his military enlistment form.

'Complexion, fresh. Eyes, blue. Hair, blond. It doesn't match the photo.'

'Now compare it to Charles's appearance.'

'Complexion, fresh. Eyes, brown. Hair, light brown,' Margaret read. 'It's him!'

'Yes. That's your grandfather, Charles Ernest Farrier. I think his name was written on the reverse of the postcard, but it was obliterated, leaving just the date.'

Margaret shook her head disbelievingly. 'But why ever would he do that?'

'I think there are clues in the two postcards that he sent Nellie. In the first one he mentions insurance and her getting his will. It could have been purely for financial reasons. Charles's early life was blighted with poverty and I guess he saw a way out.' Morton shrugged. 'Well, it worked, didn't it? She bought a house way away from their old life in Eastbourne where nobody would recognise them, then they remarried by licence, so no banns were called to alert anybody.'

'My goodness,' Margaret repeated.

'When I first saw Leonard and Nellie's marriage certificate, I spotted that their witnesses were married on the same day. I've got a feeling that Nellie and Leonard—*Charles*—just grabbed the nearest two people to witness the service. Two unknowns who wouldn't question it.'

'Golly, no wonder there are no pictures or anything belonging to Charles. That would have given the game away, wouldn't it! But that means that their other child, Alex is actually a Farrier and not a Sageman!' Margaret declared.

'Yep. Just to make the Farrier tree even more complicated.'

Margaret laughed. 'Isn't it just.'

'Did Alex have any children?'

'Yes, he had three sons. I don't know much more about what happened to them. As you know, my dad was a bit of a miserable character and once we moved to Folkestone, he didn't see much of his half-brother—or full brother as we now know him to have been.'

'It would be good to try and make contact with them; tell them all we've discovered,' Morton said.

'I'm not sure anyone would believe it, though! Can you find them?'

Morton nodded. 'Shouldn't be too tricky. There are various ways of doing it—through birth, marriage and death records, then using an electoral register search. First, though, I'd like to try a website called *Lost Cousins*. It's a great website that kind of does what it says on the tin. You put your family details in and make contact with distant relatives. I've used it before for clients on genealogical cases but have never actually inputted my own family.'

'Get on with it then! I'll go and make us a coffee.'

Morton opened up a new browser and navigated to the *Lost Cousins* website. It felt strange but exciting to create his own account, in his own name. The first step was to add known relatives into the *My*

73

Ancestors page, using a variety of censuses as a guide to ensuring a correct match with living relatives. Morton selected the 1911 English and Welsh census and, using the relevant piece and schedule number, inputted Charles Ernest Farrier's name and age. Once added, Morton clicked search.

No matches.

Morton returned to the *My Ancestors* page and inputted Nellie Ellingham's name and age. He hit the search button and waited.

1 new match found. Please check your My Cousins page.

Morton held his breath as he clicked the link. He was presented with the initials—AS, country of residence of the match—UK and connection—Nellie Ellingham. Beside the entry was a link—*make connection*. Morton hovered his cursor over the word, briefly considering the implications of what he was about to do, then clicked it. Onscreen appeared the words *Request sent 25th December 2014*. Now he just needed to sit and wait. He made up his mind when he got home to work on the Farrier family tree and add the rest of the family into the website, hopefully being able to make contact with other living relatives. One day he might even get to add his own father's family.

'Coffee!' Margaret announced, noisily setting a cup on the table beside his laptop. 'Do you know, I can't stop thinking about Grandad Farrier and Grandad Len—it's *so* bizarre. I'm itching to hear what happened on the 26th!'

'Shall I read it now?'

'No! Be strong!' Margaret rebuked with a smirk. 'Any other new developments?'

Morton smiled. 'Well, there is someone on *Lost Cousins* who is descended from Nellie. Their initials are AS.'

'Oh right, what happens now, then?'

'Now we sit and wait for AS to log in to their emails.'

'Oh golly.'

'Fancy a walk after the coffee?' Morton asked. 'It's been a bit of a heavy day, with one thing and another; I could do with some fresh air.'

'You go, I think you probably need a bit of time by yourself,' Margaret said perceptively.

Morton nodded. She was right and he had actually hoped that she would decline his invitation. It wasn't that he didn't want her company; it was simply that he needed just a few minutes by himself.

Outside, the bracing salty air blasted against his face as he ambled slowly along the cliff path. He passed the disused coastguard hut and his thoughts turned to this morning and to the new life ahead of him as a married man. He loved Juliette and wanted to spend his life with her. The happiness that she evoked in him and the calmness that her presence brought him could never be equalled. She seemed to know and comprehend his thoughts before he had even thought them. She understood and guided him gently through the turbid complex waters of his past. Right now, though, he felt like one of the tiny boats out on the open seas before him: released from the past with a whole world out in front of him.

Morton took a step up onto the grassy bank and drew in a long, deep breath. He stared out into the distance. Somewhere out there, probably on another continent, was his biological father. A normal real man who had no idea of his existence.

Jack. An American with some connection to Boston. A degree in archaeology. A stay in Folkestone in early 1974. That was the sum of his knowledge about his father. It wasn't much, but it was enough. 'Dad,' he mouthed into the air.

He closed his eyes and felt the cold wind on his face. Wind that blew in from his father's homeland.

For the first time in his life he felt part of a family with a past, present and a future.

Taking in another long inhalation, Morton headed back down the hill to join his fiancée for a drink in the pub.

Chapter Thirteen

25th December 1914, Le Hamel, France

Charles Farrier was standing in a long queue of noisy soldiers, which slowly snaked its way through the ground floor of the house towards the dining room. A temporary kitchen had been established there to serve the company Christmas dinner. Alone in his thoughts, Charles was feeling surprisingly grateful. Yesterday evening, just as the men were beginning to relax in their billets, the Battalion had been ordered to proceed at 9am on Christmas Day to relieve the 6th Brigade near Cambrin, a prospect they had all feared and which had severely dampened their evening. However, at 11.30 last night, the order had been cancelled and the men had slept well in the knowledge that their Christmas Day would be a peaceful one. The cancelled order had come with the caveat that the Battalion must be ready to move with just one hour's notice. Last night Frank and Jimmy had returned from the red lamps, slightly inebriated, dragging with them a small fir sapling. They had also procured from somewhere a few measly strips of tinsel and a handful of over-sized baubles, which looked ridiculous on the diminutive tree. *But it was better than nothing*, Charles thought, as he looked at the tree standing drunkenly in the corner of the room that he was sharing with the five other men.

They had woken to a bitingly cold bedroom and had worked quickly to ignite the brazier. Following a slow breakfast of bacon and tea, the men had sat quietly on their own beds and opened their presents from home. Carefully wrapped inside brown paper, Charles had found two pairs of thick socks, several bars of chocolate, a plum pudding, some dried fruit and a new photograph of Nellie and Alfred inside a decorative leather case.

'Here you go,' Charles had said to Leonard, tossing a small wrapped parcel at him. 'Happy Christmas.'

Leonard had looked surprised at being given the package.

'From Nellie and little Alfie. Well, and me of course.'

Leonard had opened the parcel and smiled at the gifts of socks, candles, a packet of fancy biscuits and some dried fruit. 'Thank you.'

Charles had seen in Leonard's eyes how much the trivial gifts had meant to him; without them, he would have had nothing. His aging aunt certainly wasn't going to send him anything.

Charles returned to the present when Leonard turned to speak to him. 'Smells delicious, doesn't it?' he asked.

'My stomach's doing summersaults,' Charles replied. They were in a grand, high-ceilinged room once used as a library before the house had become another casualty of war. Each wall had been lined with floor-to-ceiling bookshelves; but only a few books now remained. Small handfuls had been hastily grabbed by the exiled previous owners and half a dozen 'borrowed' by transient soldiers; the bulk that had remained had slowly kept the braziers and cooking vats burning for the past few weeks, when the claws of winter had sunk into the house. For Charles, the sight of the empty shelves, knowing that all those precious tomes had been consumed by fire, was desperately pitiful. It was just another consequence of war to which desensitised men paid no thought. Nobody whosoever even raised an eyebrow to the literary destruction. *But how could they*, Charles thought. *They had marched until their feet had bled. They had stood for hours in freezing water. They had witnessed shells ripping apart their friends and enemies. They had watched helplessly as rats had devoured their comrades' internal organs. No thing or person held any value anymore.*

Yet it broke Charles's heart as much as seeing the death of his friends. For him, it symbolised a further lowering of humanity. *If we can't even care for a pile of books*, he thought, *what hope do we have of caring for other human beings?*

Charles watched from his position in the line, as one of the three cooks began to wrench, break and snap away chunks of the actual shelving behind him. He slowly fed the pieces into the fire.

Finally reaching the front of the queue, Charles received his plate of food: boiled potatoes, carrots and a piece of chicken, all swimming in a watery brown liquid that reminded him of the stuff slopping about in the bottom of the trenches. 'Delicious,' he said flatly.

In the adjoining lounge and dining room, a variety of makeshift tables had been assembled, some covered with tablecloths and a vase of fresh flowers. The two rooms were raucous with light-hearted chatter and laughter; it was a welcome sound for Charles, as he took a seat on a long table between Leonard and Edward Partington.

'This is alright, isn't it?' Edward said cheerfully.

'Better than the alternative order where we had to spend the day relieving the Sixth,' Leonard answered, tucking into his dinner.

'But that only means that *they're* still stuck in the trenches,' Charles muttered. 'Poor buggers.'

'Rather them than me,' Edward said. 'I want to get back home in one piece. The less time I spend at the end of Fritz's gun barrels the better.'

'Hear, hear,' Leonard said, raising his glass of rum. 'Happy Christmas, folks. Let's hope we don't see another one on active service.'

'I'll drink to that,' Charles said, his glass joining the others above the table.

From the end of the room a gravely, throaty cough drew the attention of the men: conversations lulled and cutlery was placed down. Another cough and the room fell silent. Major Carmichael, standing on a wooden crate, pushed his glasses up onto the bridge of his nose. He was a short man with a generous sprouting of grey ear and nasal hair. 'Good afternoon, men,' he began in his clipped voice. 'I would just like to interrupt your meal, if I may, to say a few words. I shan't ramble on for too long. First of all, on behalf of the lieutenant colonel, I would like to express gratitude to the officers, NCOs, and men of the Royal Sussex for their fine conduct under what has proven to be very trying and difficult circumstances during these opening months of war. The regiment's diligence and dedication has not been without its losses; the *iron regiment* has suffered greatly. However, with a new year ahead of us and new blood swelling the ranks, I *know* we shall prevail in our just fight. And in recognition of the entire British Army's endeavours, you have been issued with Christmas cards from their Majesties the king and queen and also a gift sent on behalf of Princess Mary, from the nation, which I trust you shall take great pleasure in opening. All that remains now, is for me to wish you all a very pleasant Christmas Day. Orders have been received that we shall be moving off at six am tomorrow to relieve the Sixth. Happy Christmas.'

The room was instantly ignited with chatter.

'Well, that speech ended on a high note—Jesus, talk about a good way to ruin a day,' Edward complained.

'Happy Christmas one and all,' Leonard said, mimicking the major's voice. 'But tomorrow you're back at the front.'

Charles shook his head dismally and tried to filter out all extraneous thoughts so that he was left alone, imagining that he was enjoying Christmas dinner with Nellie and Alfred. He wondered what they were doing right at this very moment. He greatly hoped that they were warm, fed and happy. If that were true then he could cope with anything that the British Army threw at him.

78

The Christmas cards from the king and queen, along with the gift from Princess Mary, were distributed among the men as they ate their hot Christmas pudding.

Charles studied the card; on the front was a split picture with King George on the right and Queen Mary on the left. On the reverse of the card was a facsimile of a handwritten greeting, signed off by the two monarchs: *With our best wishes for Christmas 1914. May God protect you and bring you home safe.*

Edward held his card up to his face. 'Terribly sorry, your Majesties, but I didn't send you a card. I'll make sure I do next year, if the Hun haven't bumped me off before then, that is.'

Charles smiled and looked at the gift from Princess Mary. It was a five-inch-long brass box, embossed with an image of the princess surrounded by a laurel wreath. He opened the lid and removed the contents: a pipe, an ounce of tobacco, a packet of twenty cigarettes in a yellow monogrammed wrapper and a tinder lighter. 'Kind of her,' he muttered.

Leonard pocketed his gifts and cards. 'Come on, let's head to our room and have a sing song.'

Back in the bedroom, the men slumped down onto their beds. Outside, the light was fading. From the brazier came a ghostly yellow glow. Leonard, with his mouth organ poised, sat up and began to softly play *O Come All Ye Faithful*. Charles, along with the other men, quietly joined in, as memories of Christmases past seeped into his mind. He knew that there was a very good chance that this could be the last Christmas he ever saw. With that solemn thought in mind, he pulled out the standard army will, which he had been putting off completing in the naïve view that he would be able to survive the war. But so few of the original British army had survived the first four months of war. It was time to be realistic now.

To the sombre, dulcet tones of his comrades' singing, Charles completed his last will and testament.

'Blimey, this is all getting a bit maudlin,' Frank joked. 'How about something rousing, like *Sussex by the Sea?*'

'Good idea,' Charlie said.

Leonard began to play the opening bars of *Sussex by the Sea* and Charles quickly realised that he preferred festive melancholia to fabricated optimism and cheer. Still, he sang the full five verses along with the other men.

By silent shared agreement, the singing ended and the men lay in the beds immersed in their own thoughts.

Chapter Fourteen

25th December 1914, Beachy Head, Eastbourne, England

Nellie Farrier stood at the very edge of Beachy Head, the tips of her muddy black shoes touching the final blades of grass before the five-hundred-foot drop to the shingle and rocks below. Here she was as close to Charlie as she could possibly get. She stared out across the English Channel. Today, the skies were clear of all but the odd white wisp, and on the horizon she could see the faint coastline of France. Her eyes carefully traced the undulations in the distant hills, following as they rose and fell just like the coastline on which she was standing. Soon after finishing her Christmas dinner, which she had helped to prepare with Dorothy and Gwen, Nellie had opened her Christmas present from Charlie—a large brass shell, which he had fashioned into a vase. On the bottom, he had etched *To my darling Nellie, Christmas 1914.*

Nellie turned her head, angling her ears towards the sea. She heard nothing but a squawking from some distant seagulls. Not a single gun was firing. She smiled, knowing in her heart that if Charlie had survived the intervening days since his last letter to her, then today he should be safe. She imagined him, out there somewhere, opening the present that she had sent to him. She knew that the practical gifts of socks and food would be welcomed, but that he would most cherish the new photograph of her and the baby. *Gifts for the body and gifts for the mind,* she had thought when choosing what to send. For Nellie, the latter was the most important. After his impoverished upbringing in Lambeth, she knew that Charlie could withstand the physical anguishes and discomforts at which whispers and rumours from the front had hinted. It was his state of mind for which Nellie had always been the most concerned. She remembered his pasty face when he returned home with the inevitable confirmation that the Battalion was being posted to France to face the coming war head on. She had stood, dazed, watching as he had gathered up the few precious belongings that he had to his name. Nellie had never seen him like that before; he seemed entirely oblivious to her and her desperate pleas. He had zipped from the house and had sold and pawned everything of value, including his own parents' wedding rings, in order to procure a generous life insurance, should something happen to him whilst on active service.

'But, Charlie, you'll be alright,' Nellie had soothed when he had returned with the insurance in place. 'You've been in the army now for four years.'

Nellie remembered how adamant Charlie had been. He had shaken his head and spoken simply and clearly. 'This is different, Nell. This is going to be like nothing we've ever seen before.'

'But the papers...' she had begun.

'Forget the papers,' Charlie had interjected, a slight quiver in his voice. 'They're just saying what the government wants them to say. Look at what's going on: the whole world is lining up to fight, building tanks and war ships, like they've never done before, calling up men in their thousands. This will be a war like no other.'

Nellie had begun to cry and Charlie had leaned in and held her. What had worried her more than anything in her life, and still now worried her was her first sight of Charlie's tears, as he quietly sobbed on her shoulder.

A loud crack from somewhere over the seas jolted Nellie back to her precarious place on the cliff-top. She looked down at the waves breaking their white crests on the great chunks of rock so far below her. The narrow band of beach, that had accepted the lives of so many helpless souls, looked strangely peaceful and tranquil. For the briefest of moments, Nellie considered how easy it would be to take one step forward and make all the agony, sitting so heavily on her heart every minute of every day, simply disappear. She thought of little Alfie and took a step back. She couldn't do it to him and she couldn't do it to Charlie.

Nellie took another step back and chastised herself for being so weak. 'We will get through this wretched war,' she shouted out to the horizon. 'Me, you and Alfie—we will get through this.'

Taking in a long, steady breath of air, Nellie whispered goodbye to Charlie and began the descent from Beachy Head. She walked slowly at first, reluctant to put distance between her and her husband. Then her thoughts turned to Alfie, whom she had left in the care of Gwen and Dorothy, and her pace quickened. Although she had only been gone for an hour, the time was amplified by her lamenting Charlie's absence. She could do nothing to be closer to Charlie, but she could get home quickly, hold her baby tightly and pray.

Chapter Fifteen

Nellie was sitting on her white cast-iron chair in the shadow of the two large elder trees at the bottom of her garden. The mid-morning sun had just risen above the cottage roof, promising another blistering day. She stared at the vacant chair beside her and thought of her dear Len. It had been six weeks now since his passing. Well-meaning widowed friends from the village had passed on clichéd thoughts about her life gradually getting better with time. But she didn't have the kind of time left that could even attempt to repair the gaping hole his death had left in her life. The practical, everyday chores and responsibilities that had been solely Len's—driving, dealing with finances, reading the meters, tending to the allotment—could be overcome, but there was not sufficient time left in the world to overcome the emotional chasm created by sixty-two years of marriage, friendship and companionship.

A flash of movement caught Nellie's eye. She looked up and watched Margaret tottering down the garden path, carefully clutching a tray, her bump having grown considerably in the short space of time that she had been with her. Nellie smiled. Two weeks had passed since her arrival and her son's transparent plan of dumping Margaret on her as a means of distraction from her grief was working. Nellie had made it her mission—one final adventure—to drag her granddaughter out of herself and to prepare her for life in the world after *the event*.

'Oh, Granny, I hope these are okay. I don't think they've risen properly,' Margaret moaned, as she set down the tray containing two cups of tea and a plate of freshly baked scones.

'Nonsense, they look perfect,' Nellie remarked, taking one from the pile.

Margaret grimaced whilst she waited for her grandmother to take a bite.

'Goodness me, you've got the knack,' Nellie said. 'Cooked to perfection.'

Margaret smiled and took the empty seat beside Nellie.

Nellie sipped at her tea and nibbled the scone, aware that something was bothering Margaret. She watched as the girl stared fixatedly at the purple smoke tree at the garden's perimeter, her mind elsewhere. 'Thinking about the baby?'

Margaret shot a mournful look at her and nodded. 'Sort of. There's something I haven't said…'

'Go on.'

Margaret returned her focus to the tree and, after a few seconds' pause, mumbled the words that were troubling her. 'I wasn't attacked.'

Nellie set down her teacup and wrapped her fingers over Margaret's trembling hand, considering what she had just heard. It was obvious why she had said that she had been raped: to remove some of the judgement and prejudice that she had still faced at being pregnant at sixteen years of age. 'Does your father know?'

Margaret nodded and her eyes welled with tears. 'He made me promise never to tell anyone the truth.'

Nellie inhaled sharply. *It certainly went some way to explaining his awful attitude towards his own daughter,* she thought. 'What about your brother, does he know?'

Margaret shook her head. 'Nobody else. Just Dad…and now you,' she sobbed.

A long silence hung in the air between the two of them.

'Are you angry with me, like Dad is?' Margaret eventually said.

Nellie squeezed her hand reassuringly. 'Not one bit, my girl, not one bit.'

Margaret looked at Nellie doubtfully. 'Really?'

'You've had your reasons. What about the father, does he know?'

'He's long gone. He lives in America.'

'No chance of him coming back?'

'No.'

'I see,' Nellie said quietly.

Wiping her eyes with the back of her hand, Margaret turned to face Nellie. 'I just don't think I can keep it a secret, especially when I'll probably end up seeing the baby as it grows up.'

'This is a tricky one,' Nellie uttered. 'But I think it might be for the best, though, if you don't change your story. Hand the baby over to your brother and move on with your life as a sixteen-year-old girl.'

'But how do I keep it a secret my whole life?'

'It's possible, believe me,' Nellie said, reflecting on her own secret that she had carried with her for sixty years. The secret that she would take to her grave.

Margaret's silence allowed Nellie's mind to wander back to the dreadful day that the news of Charlie's death had arrived. A cold, impersonal form had been delivered to the house in Eastbourne. Not even a telegram, as received by the relatives of deceased officers. Nellie could still recall it with clarity. Army form B.104-82. Charlie's life whittled down to a standard form. At the top of the form was stamped the regiment and Battalion name. Below it, the handwritten word *Madam* preceded a standard typed letter. She still knew every word of it, all these years later. *It is my painful duty to inform you that a report has been received from the War Office notifying the death of:-*

There then followed a soulless mixture of stamps and handwritten words, which had told her little of what had actually befallen poor Charlie. *In the field, France* had been noted as the location. A standard expression of sympathy from the monarchs was written at the bottom of the form, before being signed off by an unidentifiable signature and the words *Officer in charge of Records.*

Despite the extraordinary events that had followed, Nellie could still feel the hollow grief that tore into her, the echo of which she could feel right now. Mercifully, she had had Gwen and Dorothy to help her through the dark days which had ensued. She had immediately ceased her trips to the cliff-tops of Beachy Head, fearing what the terrors inside her might have led her to do. In fact, her grief had led her to a dangerous, inward-looking place where her care for herself and for Alfred had slipped. It had been more than three weeks until the letter had arrived, which had caused such emotional confusion in her mind. It was a short, simple letter purportedly from Charlie's best friend, Len, telling her that she should use Charlie's enclosed will to help cash in his assurance policy and to use the money to move away from Eastbourne. At the bottom of the letter was a hand-drawn orange lily, identical to those on the bottom of Charlie's previous letters and postcards. For hours Nellie had sat in bed clutching the letter, reading it over and over again, trying to make sense of it. She had compared it to the other postcards sent by Charlie and knew then that he was alive. The handwriting was different—yes—but only very slightly; it was definitely Charlie's. Her elation at this discovery was matched by her fierce anger towards him. *How could he put me through three weeks of torment like this?* she had thought. The money she had eventually received from the insurance did little to quell her fury towards him. Days had followed where Nellie had been forced to maintain her grief for the benefit of those around her. It wasn't until she had finally moved away to Westbere that she had forgiven Charlie. She recalled that her forgiveness of him and the acceptance of their situation had occurred right here, in this very garden, when one evening she had lit a small

85

bonfire, placing on it all traces of Charlie. She had genuinely mourned him, as she tossed photographs, letters and postcards onto the pyre. With great reluctance, she even burnt the only copy of their wedding photograph. By the following morning nothing had remained of Charles Ernest Farrier, but for one sepia portrait of him in uniform. She had scribbled out his name and concealed the picture under her mattress.

Margaret's continued sobbing brought Nellie back to the present. 'Come on, this is no good. Let's pick some flowers; brighten your room up a bit.'

Margaret stood, tried to compose herself and followed Nellie over to a thick bed of orange lilies, upon which danced an array of bees and hoverflies. 'Smell that; it's simply delicious.'

'They're nice,' Margaret said softly.

'I've had them in the garden ever since I moved here in 1915. The orange lilies was the nickname for the Royal Sussex Regiment that Grandad Farrier and Grandad Len served in together. It's my little tribute.'

Margaret smiled and seemed to take more interest. 'Why were they called that?'

Nellie laughed. 'It dates back to seventeen something or other when a general parading the regiment after a military success in Quebec remarked how they look like orange lilies because their tunics were buttoned outwards, which apparently looked like the common wild lilium. As with most nicknames it stuck, even when the uniform changed.'

Margaret bent down and took a long, deep breath and thought of her beloved Grandad Len, who had treated her as though she were his real granddaughter.

Chapter Sixteen

Morton and Juliette were sitting up in bed, enjoying the cool air wafting in through the open window. Juliette was reading her book, but only half concentrating—distracted by the view across the Cadgwith bay and out to the open seas. Morton was just finishing the remnants of his breakfast in bed, which Juliette had delivered with the warning words: 'Do not—*under any circumstances*—get used to this.'

'I might take that test in a minute,' Morton said, gesturing towards the DNA kit, which sat on his bedside table, tantalising him with promises of revelations into his own ancestry.

'Go for it,' she said, still staring out the window.

Morton set aside his tray. 'You can go and wash it all up now, fiancée,' he said with a grin.

Juliette turned to face him, raised her eyebrows and pulled a *that's never going to happen* face, then returned to her book.

Morton picked up the box and carefully opened it. Inside was a sealed swab and a requisite raft of accompanying paperwork. He read all the information, filled in the necessary forms then took the saliva test and sealed the packet. 'There. Done. We'll send it off on our way home. In six to eight weeks I'll get the results.'

'Presumably you'll have a large percentage of North American DNA, then?' Juliette answered.

'Probably, yes. Unless there are any other secrets lurking in the past. Right, I suppose I'd better get up. Aunty Margaret will be chomping at the bit for me to read today's unit diary.'

'Take the tray with you and wash it all up, fiancé,' Juliette smirked.

Morton grinned and carried the tray from the room.

Downstairs, Jim was sitting by the fire reading a paper and Margaret was flicking through television channels at an alarming rate.

'Morning,' she greeted, switching the television off.

'Oh, at last,' Jim said, looking up vaguely from his paper. 'Put this poor old thing out of her misery—she's been driving me potty this morning.'

Margaret chortled. 'I couldn't sleep, either. I've not been this excited for years. You've got me proper hooked, Morton Farrier!'

'No pressure, then,' Morton said, starting up his laptop. 'Okay.'

Margaret sat perched on the edge of her chair, looking like an eager puppy. Even Jim set down his newspaper to listen to the entry.

'Twenty-sixth December. Cambrin. Moved off at 6am to the relief of the 6th Brigade near Cambrin. We commenced relieving the Staffords at 12 noon and did not finish until 8.30pm—another bad communication trench. Here we had 900 yards of trench, which we held with three companies, with one platoon in support. 'C' company, who had 90 men admitted to hospital on 24th and 25th having been distributed among the other three companies. The enemy sent over about 20 high explosives. Three rank and file missing.'

Margaret and Jim looked at each other, their disappointment clearly evident.

'Is that it?' Margaret said at last. 'I was hoping for more detail. It doesn't even mention the poor blighters' names, does it.' She shook her head. '*Rank and file.*'

Morton also couldn't help but feel disappointed, although he knew deep down that very seldom did rank and file soldiers get mentioned in the unit diaries, even when killed or captured. He looked again at the end of the entry. Three rank and file missing. One was Leonard Sageman and one his great grandfather, Charles Ernest Farrier. Morton returned to the Commonwealth War Graves Commission website and re-entered his great grandfather's name. He then clicked through to the page on Le Touret Memorial and *See Casualty Records*. On screen, Morton was presented with a list of the thirteen thousand, four hundred and fifty-five commemorated there. Charles was listed on the first page. The entry below listed the only other solider killed that day: Private Cyril Stoneham. Just like Charles, he too was commemorated at the Le Touret Memorial, also without a known grave.

'The other man was called Cyril Stoneham,' Morton told Margaret and Jim. Morton scribbled the entry onto his notepad and recapped what he knew. 'So that day, twenty high explosives were sent over, which killed Leonard Sageman and Cyril Stoneham. Charles, though, wasn't killed but managed to take Leonard's ID and somehow was captured by the Germans. It sounds to me like they weren't in the trenches when it all happened...'

'Is that really all you can find out?' Margaret said. 'You'll be going home shortly and I feel like it's all a bit of an anti-climax because we don't know the whole story.'

'Hmm,' Morton agreed. *There has to be more out there than this*, he thought. 'Don't worry, Aunty Margaret, I'll continue the case when I get back. I'll see what West Sussex Record Office and the National Archives have got on him. Also the National Army Museum is due to put all their Soldiers' Effects Records online, covering soldiers killed in the British army 1901 to 1960. Have no fear—there's plenty more to do from home!'

'Just make sure you keep me up-to-date,' she said, before ambling off into the kitchen.

Morton opened up his emails and, among the usual newsletters, junk and eBay alerts, was an email from an Andrew Sageman with the subject *Greetings!* He eagerly clicked to open the message. *Dear Morton, How lovely to hear from you! Sad that we know so little of each other's families, despite sharing such a recent common ancestor in Nellie Sageman (neé Ellingham). Nellie was my grandmother and I have very fond memories of her. Which trees are you researching? I have a great collection of information on the Ellinghams and Sagemans, though I doubt the latter will hold much of interest to you. After Nellie's funeral many of her personal effects, photos, etc. were put out for people to help themselves to. As a keen family historian, I took everything that nobody else wanted! What might be of interest to you are a few bits and pieces regarding Nellie's first husband, Charlie. Somewhere (!) I have his original 1914 will, his war medals, his original pay pocket book (complete with blood stains) and a letter, including a brief account of Charlie's last movements from his friend, Edward Partington. If any of this is of interest, please let me know and I'll have a rummage and get it copied for you! Best wishes, Andrew Sageman.*

'Wow! Come and look at this, Aunty Margaret,' he called excitedly.

She darted into the room and read over his shoulder. 'Golly. So this is the person you found on that *Lost Cousins* website, is it?'

'That's right. Do you know him?'

Margaret screwed up her face. 'Yes, but no. As kids we were often all at Granny's house for parties, Christmas, that kind of thing but once Granny died it all fizzled out. I haven't seen Andrew for donkey's years.'

'I'll email him straight back and ask him if he could send me copies of everything he has for Charles. Then I might tell him about our discoveries. Not sure how that'll go down...'

'So we might yet find out what happened to Grandad Len and Grandad Farrier that day,' Margaret mused.

'Let's hope so,' Morton answered absent-mindedly, tapping out a short reply. 'Well, I suppose Juliette and I should think about packing soon. We've got a long trip back to Sussex ahead of us. We're going to stop off at Dad's to tell him our good news. Jeremy and Guy are staying with him and apparently they forced him to eat a Christmas dinner yesterday, which is a miracle.'

Margaret laughed. 'A load of old commercial nonsense,' she said, impersonating her brother. 'I think he's getting soft in his old age—I even had a Christmas card from him this year.'

'Wonders will never cease,' Morton said, shutting down his laptop.

Just over an hour later, Morton and Juliette were standing in the lounge, pulling on their shoes and coats. Their two packed suitcases stood by the front door.

'Right,' Morton began, fearing an awkward silence was about to expand into the room, 'it's been…amazing. Thank you for having us to stay; we've had a lovely time. Thanks, Uncle Jim, for putting up with all the genealogy.'

'Well, it's kept Margaret quiet—that's no easy feat,' he said, offering his hand to Morton.

Morton shook his uncle's hand then turned and embraced his Aunty Margaret.

'Thank you for your understanding, Morton,' she whispered. 'Good luck with your future quests. I hope you find him.'

'Thanks,' Morton replied softly.

'Goodbye, nearly-niece-in-law,' Jim roared, scooping Juliette into his arms.

'Put the poor girl down, James,' Margaret said. 'Goodbye, dear. It's been lovely to get to know you. Welcome to the family.'

'Thank you both so much—it's obviously been a really important visit for us, for a variety of reasons. Thanks,' Juliette said.

'You're welcome down here anytime,' Margaret added.

With Margaret and Jim watching and waving from the front porch, Morton and Juliette walked hand in hand down the path towards the Mini.

Morton heaved the suitcases into the boot then slumped into the driver's seat. He faced Juliette and smiled. 'We did it.'

'*You* did it,' she replied.He had done it. In five short days he had confronted his past and accepted his future. 'Come on then, let's get back to Sussex.'

Chapter Seventeen

26ᵗʰ December 1914, Cambrin, France. 9.15pm.

Charles Farrier was standing poised in the fire trench, ankle-deep in mud with Leonard Sageman, failing to suppress a shiver nipping the length of his spine. Both men stood silently waiting for a third man to join them before going over the parapet to check the wire. It was a routine job that Charles had undertaken before now and which had not particularly fazed him on those occasions; tonight, however, the brightness of the moon troubled him. Sergeant Buggler, who had given the order, had assured him that it was still too subdued to be useful to guide enemy fire.

Charles glanced down at himself. His new socks and clean clothes were already unrecognisable through the wet solid covering of fetid mud. He looked up and was immediately displeased to see Cyril Stoneham standing in front of Sergeant Buggler, having been selected as the third member of their party. *Of all the people to accompany us over the top, it has to be that obtuse profane man,* Charles thought.

'Okay, boys. Off you go. Be quick about it,' the sergeant growled.

'Good luck, lads,' Edward Partington called, as he watched them one by one ascend the wooden ladder over the parapet. As they scrambled up to a standing position, each man held his breath in anticipation of sudden enemy fire; all of them had a catalogued history of knowing men who had been sniped at exactly such a moment. Instinctively, they all stood still for a moment, surveying the brutal landscape around them. To Charles, each time he saw No Man's Land up close like this, it grew more and more unrecognisable. No longer part of France. No longer part of Europe. No longer part of the world. Just desolate and barren, where the only living things were parasitic vermin, preying on the expiring pulses of nationless men. The crescent moon, sitting low in the open skies among a smattering of stars, only served to render the land starker, more monochromatic.

'Come on then,' Charles whispered to the two men, his breath puffing out into the chilled air. He led them on the most direct course that he could find, zigzagging past rotting body parts, water-filled craters and stumps of wood that were once trees, all the while fighting against the unyielding adhesive drag and suction from the mud below.

'Hang on a sec,' Stoneham called after a few minutes' walking, bending double to catch his breath.

Leonard and Charles continued a few paces then stopped, also grateful for a short break.

'Hello, Fritz!' Stoneham suddenly said loudly, standing up and heading to a nearby crater.

'Shut up!' Charles hissed, searching for the focus of Stoneham's attention.

'What are you doing?' Leonard glowered.

'Calm down,' Stoneham called back. 'Just saying hi to Fritz, here.'

With a clear shaft of moonlight reflecting back from the water, Charles could see a dead German solider hanging out of the crater, his body slumped to the side, as if he ran out of life trying to free himself from his watery grave.

'For God's sake, leave him alone,' Charles called back, needing to express his absolute disapproval but also feeling uncomfortable with how their voices would be carrying across the bleak landscape.

'Let's go and get him,' Leonard whispered to Charles. 'Damned fool that he is.'

The two men hurried as quickly as they could towards Stoneham, who was rifling through the dead German's pockets.

'What are you doing?' Leonard demanded. 'Leave the poor bugger alone.'

Charles studied the German's face. He was young; he could only have been in his early twenties with a good-looking defined face. Under his *Pickelhaube* Charles could see cropped dark hair. His eyes were closed and, despite the incongruous surroundings, he actually looked peaceful.

Stoneham examined a small book that he had pulled out from the soldier's pocket. 'Say hello to Gustav,' he said, waving the book in the air. As he did so, something fell to the floor, landing by Charles's right foot. Charles stooped down to pick it up. He held it close to his face and saw that it was a photograph of the dead German in full military uniform with a young baby girl, around the same age as Alfie, sitting on his knee. Charles turned the photograph over and read the inscription. *Für meinen Papa mit Liebe, Anna xx*

'Put it back,' Charles instructed, watching incredulously as Stoneham began to work a ring from the soldier's finger.

'Stop!' Leonard shouted, but Stoneham was oblivious. 'I'm going to report you when we get back.'

Stoneham stopped, looked up at Len and was about to answer when the German soldier suddenly lifted his head and gasped a giant lungful of air.

Stoneham yelped loudly and fell backwards.

The unmistakable crack of a single rifle-shot resounded in the air, a split-second before a bullet smashed into Leonard's chest, sending him crashing backwards, landing with a thud and squelch.

Charles dropped to his knees and crawled over to Len.

Another crack rang into the sky and Stoneham tumbled backwards into the crater with the gasping German, a bullet having pierced into his right thighbone.

'Help me!' Stoneham squealed, thrashing about in the water, trying to grasp onto the slippery edge of the crater. 'I've been hit!'

Charles ignored his pleas and gently lifted Leonard's head into his lap. His eyes were open but his face was motionless, frozen. Charles placed his ear close to Leonard's mouth: nothing. Tearing open Leonard's blood-soaked greatcoat and tunic, Charles revealed the bullet wound, glistening and gurgling like an unstoppable oil eruption. Charles placed his palm over the wound but knew that it was useless. His oldest friend, with whom he had experienced so much, was dead. He looked down at the aluminium identity tag, lying limply on Leonard's bare bloodied chest.

'Please, help me!' Stoneham pleaded, still trying to drag himself free from the crater. Watching numbly from the other side of the crater was Gustav, who had drawn on some inner strength and was mumbling in German at Stoneham, but not making any attempt to free himself.

As he surveyed the scene before him, Charles realised that he was still holding the photograph of the German soldier with his daughter. He looked again at the picture, then from the German to Stoneham. Inside his brain, so dreadfully tired of this war, something clicked into place, clear and stark: it was the image of his own dead body, forever confined to French soil, on top of which lay the photograph of Nellie and baby Alfred. *How unimportant our names are*, Charles suddenly realised. The image in his mind was shattered by Stoneham's pathetic cries.

'I swear to God, Farrier—if you don't get me out of here right now!' Stoneham yelled through the pain searing into his leg.

Charles looked from Stoneham's pitiable attempts to scramble out of the crater down to Len's cold face and at last, something made sense. Kissing Leonard on the forehead, he carefully laid him down in the mud and then took a deep breath. 'Forgive me, Len,' he mumbled, as he removed the identity tag from around Leonard's neck. Delving into his breast pocket, Charles retrieved Leonard's pay book and swapped it with his own. Charles placed his own identity tag on Leonard's chest then turned towards the two men, so desperately helpless in the crater. With his help, one of them could survive.

Trudging on his hands and knees, with mud reaching up to his elbows, Charles reached the side of the crater.

'At long bloody last, Farrier,' Stoneham shouted. 'It's my leg. It's pretty bad—I can't walk. You'll have to drag me back.'

Charles ignored his pleas and continued around the crater towards the German soldier, who sat slumped in the water, having accepted his fate. 'Here,' he said, wiping a hand on his greatcoat and pulling out the photograph of Gustav with his daughter.

'*Danke*,' he replied quietly.

'What the hell are you doing?' Stoneham yelled.

Charles offered his hand to the German.

'*Was machst du?*' the soldier asked.

'Let me help you, Gustav,' Charles said, nodding towards his hand. 'Take my hand—I'll get you out.'

'*Ich kann nicht...*' he replied, shaking his head.

'What the hell are you doing?' Stoneham repeated. 'Leave him, get me out!'

Charles drew closer to Gustav and foisted his hands under his armpits and began to drag.

A rush of realisation prompted a wave of adrenalin to pump through Stoneham's veins. He dived across the crater and began to claw at the German soldier, pulling him back into the water.

Gustav cried out in pain, as limbs and torso were wrenched and tugged in opposing directions.

Charles kept pulling, using all of his remaining strength to defy the enveloping mire and Stoneham's desperate pulls, but it was no use. The German's dead weight, combined with Stoneham's heaving was too much for Charles, who had little strength left in his arms. Reluctantly, he let Gustav go, allowing him to slide backwards, the water rising up to his chin.

With frantic fear rising in his eyes, Stoneham knew that the only way to save himself was to kill the German. He knew it would take little effort and pulled him under the surface.

All Charles could see of Gustav was a flapping and flailing of his arms above the water, as his body began to yield to the inevitable.

'Let him go,' Charles ordered, lifting his Lee-Enfield rifle, preparing to shoot.

'You wouldn't dare,' Stoneham countered, continuing his hold on the German. 'You'll be shot for this, Farrier.'

Charles carefully took aimed with his rifle and shot, the bullet whizzing past Stoneham's face, embedding itself in the bank of the crater.

It was enough.

Stoneham released his grip on Gustav.

Charles tossed down his rifle and hauled the German out of the water. He coughed and gasped; he was alive.

Stoneham sank back and watched numbly as Charles began to lug Gustav from the crater. Moments later he was free, and Charles could see the extent of Gustav's injuries: his left leg was almost separated at the knee; only a strip of cloth acting as a tourniquet tied across his thigh had stopped him from bleeding to death, though he was close to it.

Charles took a fleeting glance at Len, then began to drag the soldier across No Man's Land, inch by painful inch. Behind him, he could hear Stoneham clawing at the mud, desperately trying to reach Charles's abandoned rifle.

As Charles stepped over what appeared to be a human hand, he tried not to think of the consequences of his actions, or the likelihood of his even surviving his reckless plan. He knew, though, that if he could just survive the next few minutes, he could survive the war and be reunited with Nellie and baby Alfred, just like Gustav would be reunited with his daughter.

A single crack of rifle fire resounded across No Man's Land.

Charles flung himself down onto Gustav, unsure of the direction the bullet was headed. It landed nearby and Charles realised then that Stoneham must have achieved the crawl over to his rifle.

Another crack and Charles flinched and cried out as a bullet impacted into his thigh.

If he wanted to live, he needed to move, despite the acute burning in his leg and a severe lack of energy.

A sudden flash and bang, louder and brighter than Charles had ever experienced before, ripped open the ground behind him. Charles collapsed back down onto Gustav as they both turned to see the spectacle behind them. A massive shell had landed exactly on the crater where they had been just a few minutes ago.

Stoneham's threats ceased.

Charles propped himself up and began to drag Gustav onward. Breathless and sweating, Charles came within a few feet of the German trenches, the sinuous lines of chalk mounds glistening in the moonlight. From the animated babble emanating in front of him, he knew that he had been spotted and was being carefully observed. His movements now were slow and deliberate; his energy was almost gone.

With nothing left inside him, Charles raised both hands in the air and slumped down beside Gustav.

'*Danke mein Freund, wir werden um Sie kümmern,*' Gustav whispered. He offered Charles his hand. '*Schmidt, Gustav.*'

'Farrier, Charlie,' he mimicked, shaking the man's hand, before falling back into the mud and staring up at the moonlit sky. Behind him, he could hear the advance of a group of German soldiers.

In his head, *Sussex by the Sea* began to play. At first he hummed, then he sang aloud. 'Far o'er the seas we wander, wide thro' the world we roam; Far from the kind hearts yonder, far from our dear old home; But ne'er shall we forget, my boys, and true we'll ever be, to the girls so kind that we left behind, in Sussex by the Sea.'

Chapter Eighteen

25th September 1974, Westbere, Kent, England

Nellie paced the length of the lounge floor, back and forth, trying to subdue her nerves. Beads of sweat rose on her forehead, partly due to her anxieties and partly due to the roaring fire, so incongruous to the warm day outside. She strode towards the front window, stopped and flung it wide open. She breathed deeply and tried to steady her mind. *Maybe I'm too old for one last adventure like this,* Nellie fretted. She looked out at the three-wheeled bicycle propped up against the cottage wall. She was sure that it was exactly the same bicycle that Mrs Blake had used since her arrival in the village in the early 1950s. Since then, in her own formidable way, Mrs Blake had delivered most children from the surrounding villages. But now her services as the district midwife were quickly diminishing, as expectant mothers were being encouraged to choose the specialist maternity unit at the Kent and Canterbury Hospital. When Nellie had raised the question of delivery to Alfred, he had unequivocally insisted that Margaret deliver at home. Nellie could only surmise that the decision was entirely driven by a desire to minimise public scandal, with little consideration for Margaret's wellbeing.

Nellie looked at the grandfather clock. Mrs Blake had been upstairs with Margaret now for over two hours. The last communication—an order for hot water and an igniting of the fire ready to burn the placenta—had been more than half an hour ago. *It must almost be over,* she reasoned. *Time to phone Alfred.*

She slowly walked into the hallway and reluctantly picked up the receiver and dialled her son's number.

'Hello?' he snapped.

'Alfie, it's me,' Nellie breathed quietly. 'It's happening. Mrs Blake is with her now.'

'Is it born?' Alfred demanded.

'Not yet—any moment I should think.'

'I'm in the middle of important business; I told you to telephone me when it was over—not *during*.'

'Why are you being so harsh towards her?' Nellie responded, beginning to lose patience with her son's reprehensible attitude. She heard an exasperated sigh at the other end.

'Look, what would you have me do? Place a birth announcement in the *Folkestone Herald* for all the world to see? Celebrate my daughter's disgusting promiscuity?'

'That's enough, Alfred,' Nellie chided. Yet again, she wondered how the genes from Alfred's placid father and her had resulted in such an intolerant, irascible man, although she knew deep down that his change in attitude had occurred in the dark days following his wife's death in childbirth. She guessed that Margaret's being in labour brought back memories he would rather forget. Nellie took a deep breath. *I need to show him patience,* she thought.

'You wouldn't be so easy-going if you knew what she'd been up to...' Alfred muttered heatedly.

Nellie turned her head so that she was facing away from the stairs and lowered her voice to a whisper. 'If you're referring to the fact that she consented to this chap from America, then I know full well what she's been up to.' Nellie exhaled, instantly regretting having divulged her knowledge to him.

A pause from the other end was followed by Alfred's angry voice. 'And in America he can bloody well stay. I've written and told him so, too. Sending letters to my daughter. I've intercepted, read and destroyed every single one. Disgusting, at her age.'

A short familiar squeak from upstairs told Nellie that Margaret's bedroom door had just been opened. Without another word, she placed the receiver back down and looked expectantly upstairs.

Mrs Blake, her blue uniformed sleeves rolled to her elbows, began to cautiously descend the stairs, cradling to her chest what looked like a small bundle of fresh white blankets. With an unusual smile, Mrs Blake handed the bundle to Nellie. 'A boy.'

Warm tears of joy filled Nellie's eyes, as she cradled her great grandson. *What will become of you, my boy?* she wondered. *Hopefully you will never learn of the many Farrier family secrets that you've been born into.*

Epilogue

It was early in the morning and still dark outside. The closing of the front door jolted Morton awake, as Juliette left for work. As had happened the previous two days, he had been unable to stay asleep, wondering if an email had yet arrived back from Andrew Sageman. Morton was becoming so desperate to hear from him that last night he had composed an email, politely checking if he had sent anything, which might have gone missing. Juliette had told him to stop being so impatient and he had saved it into his drafts folder.

Morton picked up his phone from the bedside table and checked his emails. 'Yes!' he yelled, leaping from his bed. He could easily have opened the attachments on his phone but he wanted to be able to appreciate them fully and clearly, so he dashed up to his study and switched on his laptop.

Moments later, the email from Andrew Sageman was open in front of him. *Dear Morton, I have located the relevant bits and pieces from the millions of box files and folders scattered around my house and have scanned them in high resolution—hopefully it won't unduly clog up your inbox! Please let me know if there are any problems. It would be good to meet up sometime, if you would like. Perhaps it's time our two families became a bit closer? I look forward to hearing from you. Regards, Andrew.*

Morton looked at the screen, considering the email. He would dearly love to meet up with Andrew and bring the two sides of the family together again, especially given that they were more closely related than anyone had previously realised. He had decided that he needed to break the news about Charles's having taken Leonard Sageman's identity face to face. It was too much of a bombshell, which required too much evidence for an email. He would contact him again and arrange a get-together. For now, though, he had the email attachments to delve into. The first, Charles Farrier's will, Morton skimmed through quickly, being as it was an exact copy of the one he had already downloaded. The next attachment was a photograph of Charles's war medals. The three medals, appearing to be bronze, silver and gold dangling from their attached ribbons, were the standard three affectionately known to veterans as Pip, Squeak and Wilfred. That Charles was issued the 1914 Star rather than the 1914-15 Star was a nod towards his having been in service as a part of the pre-war British army.

After clicking on the next attachment, Morton was taken aback. It was a small and simple rust-coloured book with black type. *Army Book 64. Soldier's pay book for use on active service.* The photograph of the book had been taken on a white background and the book tilted to show the sides of the yellowing pages within. Despite the long passage of time which had since elapsed, the book was unequivocally stained with dried blood. *To whom did the blood belong?* Morton wondered. *Was it Charlie's, Leonard's or someone else's?* He hoped that the final document, the letter from Charles's friend, Edward Partington, might shed some light.

With a slight trepidation, although he couldn't quite fathom why, Morton read the handwritten letter to Nellie, with what the British military had taken to be the official account of Charles Ernest Farrier's last moments. *January 1915. Dear Mrs Farrier, I hope you do not find it misplaced that I write you a line about your husband and my friend, Charlie. He was such a good man, soldier and companion that I felt I should write to explain, as fully as I can, the circumstances surrounding his untimely death. On the 26th December, Charlie, Len and another chap, Stoneham, were sent out to check the wire perimeter. I was with him when he went over the top, one of the last to see him alive. They had been out only a few minutes when sniper shots were heard—two or possibly more. It is the sergeant's thinking that Charlie and Stoneham were mortally wounded. I'm dreadfully sorry to say that a mortar was fired from the enemy trenches, landing close by to where the men fell, before we had a chance to recover the bodies. Len Sageman is still missing. We are hopeful that he is alive, somehow having survived the attack. I hope that the knowledge that Charlie was well-liked and respected among the Battalion and that he died honouring his country will bring some ease to your suffering. Your friend, Edward Partington.*

Morton sat back, having read the account of Charles's—or Leonard's, as it had turned out to be—final moments. He wondered at the timing of the letter—January 1915—and whether she had already made the discovery that her husband was in fact still alive, or whether this letter from Edward Partington had added to her grief, with its likely ineffective attempts at easing her pain.

Morton looked up to the wall above his desk, where he had placed a picture of his great grandfather in his First World War uniform. From the research that he had conducted into Charles Farrier, Morton believed that his motives for taking on his best friend's identity had been motivated by money—an attempt to lift his family finally out of the poverty that had blighted it for generations in London. In doing

100

that much, he had succeeded. And, unlike so many millions of men, he had returned home at the end of the war to his wife and son.

Below the picture of Charles Farrier, was a hand-drawn Farrier family tree. Although he had wanted the neatness of a computer-generated GEDCOM file, he couldn't for the life of him figure out how to input all the peculiarities of his odd family. His eyes fell upon his great grandfather, Charles Ernest Farrier, and his great grandmother, Nellie Ellingham, and he momentarily considered all that he had learned about them in the last few days before moving down the tree to his grandfather, Alfred Farrier, and his grandmother, Anna. During his recent visit to Cornwall, his Aunty Margaret had told him that her mother, Anna, had been the daughter of a long-standing family friend, Gustav Schmidt, whom Charles—posing as Len—had got to know during the war. From Alfred and Anna, a vertical line descended and split to his adoptive father and Aunty Margaret. Finally, his eyes rested on his own name at the bottom of the tree.

'My weird and wonderful family,' he said with a smile, pencilling in the words *Juliette Meade* beside his.

Historical Information

The movements and locations of the Second Battalion Royal Sussex Regiment have been recorded as faithfully and accurately as possible. The unit diaries used are exactly as written, with the exception of the final lines from 26th December 1914; to my knowledge no soldiers were sent out to check the wire that night, and none were killed.

All characters in the book are entirely fictional, although approximate numbers of soldiers (on both sides) killed, injured and wounded are mirrored in the book. The Second Battalion of the Royal Sussex Regiment had lost 257 men by Christmas 1914 and more than 1,700 by the time of the Armistice in 1918.

All of the records that Morton uses in his research are real.

For a detailed account of The Royal Sussex Regiment's movements on the Western Front 1914-1918, see *We Won't Be Druv* by Hugh Miller.

Further information

Website: www.nathandylangoodwin.com
Twitter: @nathangoodwin76
Facebook: www.facebook.com/nathandylangoodwin
Pinterest: www.pinterest.com/dylan0470/
Blog: theforensicgenealogist.blogspot.co.uk

Praise for *Hiding the Past*
(The Forensic Genealogist #1)

'Flicking between the present and stories and extracts from the past, the pace never lets up in an excellent addition to this unique genre of literature' *Your Family Tree*

'At times amusing and shocking, this is a fast-moving modern crime mystery with genealogical twists. The blend of well fleshed-out characters, complete with flaws and foibles, will keep you guessing until the end' *Family Tree*

'Once I started reading *Hiding the Past* I had great difficulty putting it down - not only did I want to know what happened next, I actually cared' *Lost Cousins*

'This is a must read for all genealogy buffs and anyone who loves a good mystery with a jaw dropping ending!' *Baytown Genealogy Society*

'This is a good read and will appeal to anyone interested in family history. I can thoroughly recommend it' *Cheshire Ancestor*

'*Hiding the Past* is a suspenseful, fast-paced mystery novel, in which the hero is drawn into an intrigue that spans from World War II to the present, with twists and turns along the way. The writing is smooth and the story keeps moving along so that I found it difficult to put down' *The Archivist*

Praise for *The Lost Ancestor*
(The Forensic Genealogist #2)

'If you enjoy a novel with a keen eye for historical detail, solid writing, believable settings and a sturdy protagonist, *The Lost Ancestor* is a safe bet. Here British author Nathan Dylan Goodwin spins a riveting genealogical crime mystery with a pulsing, realistic storyline' *Your Family Tree*

'Finely paced and full of realistic genealogical terms and tricks, this is an enjoyable whodunit with engaging research twists that keep you guessing until the end. If you enjoy genealogical fiction and Ruth Rendell mysteries, you'll find this a pleasing page-turner' *Family Tree*

'...an extremely well-constructed plot, with plenty of intrigue and genealogical detail - but all the loose ends are neatly tied up by the end...*The Lost Ancestor* is highly recommended' *Lost Cousins*

'It's an excellent pick for holidays, weekend relaxing, or curling up indoors or outdoors, whatever the weather permits in your corner of the world' *Lisa Louise Cooke*

'*The Lost Ancestor* is fast-paced, not plodding, and does well building mystery... The author's depictions of scenes and places are vivid; the characters are interesting and intriguing. In toggling back and forth from past to present, Goodwin shows how the deeds of long-dead ancestors are haunting their descendants' *GenealogyMagazine.com*

'It's entertaining, and passes the time nicely while setting the chores aside... just the right kind of light reading we need during this time of holiday busyness' *Eastman's Online Genealogy*

Praise for *The America Ground*
(The Forensic Genealogist #4)

'As in the earlier novels, each chapter slips smoothly from past to present, revealing murderous events as the likeable Morton uncovers evidence in the present, while trying to solve the mystery of his own paternity. Packed once more with glorious detail of records familiar to family historians, *The America Ground* is a delightfully pacey read' *Family Tree*

'Like most genealogical mysteries this book has several threads, cleverly woven together by the author - and there are plenty of surprises for the reader as the story approaches its conclusion. A jolly good read!' *Lost Cousins*

'Goodwin's stories have been good reads, engaging the interest of the genealogist with references to records...Readers will welcome this new book as a welcome distraction from the intensity of research to reading about someone else's work, with murder thrown in' *Eastman's Online Genealogy Newsletter*

'Great reading - a real page-turner! Good solid genealogy research – highly recommended' *Genealogy Happy Hour*

'It's just a terrific book! It's great stuff, I've read it, and you're going to enjoy it' *Extreme Genes*

'The writing is pin-sharp and there is plenty of suspense in an excellent novel which makes me want to return to the first books in the series' *The Norfolk Ancestor*

'This is a good crime novel with links to family history and in it you have the best of both worlds...the twisting story will keep you guessing to the last page' *The Wakefield Kinsman*

Made in the USA
Charleston, SC
25 November 2016